Dance of Desire

Also from Christopher Rice

Thrillers
A DENSITY OF SOULS
THE SNOW GARDEN
LIGHT BEFORE DAY
BLIND FALL
THE MOONLIT EARTH

Supernatural Thrillers
THE HEAVENS RISE
THE VINES

Paranormal Romance
THE FLAME: A Desire Exchange Novella
THE SURRENDER GATE: A Desire Exchange Novel
KISS THE FLAME: A Desire Exchange Novella

Contemporary Romance
DANCE OF DESIRE
DESIRE & ICE: A MacKenzie Family Novella

Dance of Desire

By Christopher Rice

1001 Dark Nights

EVIL EYE
CONCEPTS

Dance of Desire
By Christopher Rice

1001 Dark Nights
Copyright 2016 Christopher Rice
ISBN: 978-1-942299-25-7

Foreword: Copyright 2014 M. J. Rose
Published by Evil Eye Concepts, Incorporated

Acknowledgments

Once again, a huge thanks to both Liz Berry and M.J Rose for inviting me to be part of this special project. (And Steve Berry for being the instigator.) Another huge thanks to Jillian Stein for making romanceland a better place with her personality, humor and social media saavy.

Kimberly Guidroz and "Shy" Pam Jamison did a wonderful job of editing this one, as always. But Kim, in particular, deserves more thanks than one page can accommodate, for more reasons than I can list here. As always, Asha Hossain does a wonderful job with the Dark Nights covers. Two more big rounds of thanks to cover model Jamison Murphy and photographer Cathryn Farnsworth.

For her friendship and general support of my romantic endeavors, I will always be grateful for the fact that Lexi Blake lives and breathes and is so generous with her knowledge and talent. And in the case of this particular novella, I'm eternally indebted to Liliana Hart, who not only invited me to write a story set in the world of her MacKenzie Family, she allowed me to crossover some of its characters into DANCE OF DESIRE.

And I'd be remiss if I didn't also give shout outs to my good friends and general support network, Eric Shaw Quinn, Becket Ghiotto, Christina Barnett, Karen O'Brien and my mother. And of course, all my Texas relatives who inspired the finer parts of this story.

One Thousand And One Dark Nights

Once upon a time, in the future...

*I was a student fascinated with stories and learning.
I studied philosophy, poetry, history, the occult, and
the art and science of love and magic. I had a vast
library at my father's home and collected thousands
of volumes of fantastic tales.*

*I learned all about ancient races and bygone
times. About myths and legends and dreams of all
people through the millennium. And the more I read
the stronger my imagination grew until I discovered
that I was able to travel into the stories... to actually
become part of them.*

*I wish I could say that I listened to my teacher
and respected my gift, as I ought to have. If I had, I
would not be telling you this tale now.
But I was foolhardy and confused, showing off
with bravery.*

*One afternoon, curious about the myth of the
Arabian Nights, I traveled back to ancient Persia to
see for myself if it was true that every day Shahryar
(Persian: شهريار, "king") married a new virgin, and then
sent yesterday's wife to be beheaded. It was written
and I had read, that by the time he met Scheherazade,
the vizier's daughter, he'd killed one thousand
women.*

*Something went wrong with my efforts. I arrived
in the midst of the story and somehow exchanged
places with Scheherazade – a phenomena that had
never occurred before and that still to this day, I
cannot explain.*

*Now I am trapped in that ancient past. I have
taken on Scheherazade's life and the only way I can
protect myself and stay alive is to do what she did to
protect herself and stay alive.*

*Every night the King calls for me and listens as I spin tales.
And when the evening ends and dawn breaks, I stop at a
point that leaves him breathless and yearning for more.
And so the King spares my life for one more day, so that
he might hear the rest of my dark tale.*

*As soon as I finish a story... I begin a new
one... like the one that you, dear reader, have before
you now.*

Prologue

Then

Amber resists, but finally opens her eyes.

Caleb really is kneeling next to her bed, whispering her name.

This isn't just another one of the sexy, grown-up dreams she's been having about the boy since summer started. Dreams in which he traces the curves of her body with his fingertips and gazes into her eyes with that serious expression that always makes him look so manly and handsome.

He's really here, his breath soft against her cheek as he whispers her name.

The smell of his cologne is as strong as all the other woodsy smells inside her father's lake house. A few hours ago, they'd both gone to bed at the same time. He in one room, she in another. So did he spritz himself before appearing at her bedside? The idea of him doing a little grooming before calling on her in the middle of the night makes her face feel tingly and hot.

The brand is probably Ralph Lauren Polo, but never would she ask because then he'll know just how much she likes it. Every whiff makes her envision the parts of his body that have become impossible to ignore, no matter how many times she tries to avert her eyes from his new biceps and his suddenly thick and powerful legs. That cologne is the aroma of his undeniable manhood. And the smell of it at her bedside makes her head spin.

They're only fifteen, but already the son of her father's best friend is over six feet tall, prompting her dad to cry more than once this trip, "Boy, you don't quit growin', you're going to be brushing the clouds by the time you're a man." That's the Caleb she's started to dream about, a powerful giant of a man, his back ridged with muscle, his solid arms powerful enough to lift her off her feet and make her feel like she's flying.

She whispers his name. But that's all she says. She doesn't want to scare him away.

Late night television drones in the living room downstairs. Her dad must have nodded off in front of the thing again.

Was that what Caleb was waiting for? For her father to fall asleep?

"It's happening," he says, taking her hand in his. "Come see!"

He tugs on her hand as she stumbles out of bed, stops long enough for her to slide her flip-flops on without releasing his grip. He waits patiently, making her feel even warmer inside.

Together they pad silently down the carpeted stairs, through the living room lit only by television flicker.

She was right; her father's out cold in his favorite recliner.

Caleb opens the sliding deck door, then once they're outside, kissed by warm air and surrounded by cricket song, he slides it shut behind them with barely a squeak. The whole time, he doesn't let go of her hand. Amber's not sure what's making her heart race—his persistent grip, or the sight of him so cheerful and excited in spite of all the trouble that's descended over his family that summer.

She doesn't know the whole story, but she's overheard some of her father's phone calls these past few days. He's used words like *detox* and *rehab* and *men who can't come back from over there*. She knows *over there* means Iraq, and she's pretty sure the man in question is Mr. Tim, Caleb's father, her dad's closest friend from the Marines. Things must've gotten bad lately. Her father plans these lake house trips weeks in advance, especially if Caleb and his dad are coming.

This trip was last minute. This time they only brought Caleb.

Whatever it is, Caleb's not talking about it.

He's not much of a talker in general and when he does open his mouth, it's usually to give soft-spoken lectures about stuff he's seen on science shows, like how volcanoes form and birds migrate. Sometimes the topic doesn't interest her that much. What interests her is how Caleb gazes into her eyes while he explains another nerdy factoid. It's like he needs for her to listen, needs for her to know what he likes. Needs for her to look into his eyes too. Just the other day, he placed one hand between her shoulder blades because he didn't want her to miss the sight of a duck skimming the lake's surface as it came in for a landing. She didn't want him to stop touching her so she just kept nodding and watching, as if landing ducks were the most interesting things ever.

They keep walking through the dark.

He's taking her to the lake.

Last spring her father replaced the steps leading down to the boathouse, and when the air is thick with humidity, like tonight, the waft of cedar comes off them in overpowering waves. The closer they get to the shore, the faster Caleb goes and the harder she has to work to keep him from pulling her off her feet.

Whatever he wants her to see, it'll be gone in a few minutes if they don't hurry.

When they reach the tip of the boathouse, he releases her hand. He's behind her suddenly, gripping her shoulder in one hand, pointing to the night sky with the other. A full moon, bursting with light, sends rivulets of ivory across the lake's black surface. This is exactly the scene he described to her earlier when they were pretending to sunbathe on the dock while sneaking looks at each other's half-naked bodies.

"What time was it last night when you saw the moon?" she'd asked him.

"Past midnight."

"But you only went to bed at eleven."

"I couldn't sleep."

They both knew what thoughts were keeping him awake, thoughts of his father's drinking and of how crazy his mother was going trying to rein it all in.

"Wake me up next time," she'd told him. *"I'll keep you company."*

Such simple words, but she'd felt like she was jumping off the edge of a cliff when she'd said them. Instead of answering, Caleb gave her a long look as he fiddled with the leg of his shorts. She'd silently cursed herself, called herself an idiot and worse.

Caleb was just a friend. Honestly, he wasn't even that, was he? Circumstances had thrown them together, that was all. He was the son of her father's best friend, so they were basically like distant cousins, only with no shared blood in their veins. Crazy of her to think there might be more there.

If her friends could see her now, they'd probably laugh at her; the same friends who'd swooned that day her father had picked her up from school with Caleb in the passenger seat of his truck, and Caleb, wearing a Stetson that was about a half-size too big for his head, had given them a cocky grin, looked right into her eyes and said, *Afternoon, pretty lady.* Not afternoon *pretty ladies,* even though she'd had about four other girls standing on the curb next to her when he'd said it.

Clearly she'd made way too much of that moment. Sometimes *afternoon* just meant, *afternoon* and *pretty lady* was what a guy called you when he was trying to look cool.

Or so she'd thought earlier that day. Before he took her up on her offer and woke her up in the middle of the night so they could look at the moon together.

Which they do.

Because it's beautiful.

When he lowers his right hand, the same hand with which he was just pointing to the night sky, her breath catches. Every muscle in her body tenses in anticipation.

Where will it land?

Her shoulder, it seems.

She forces herself to breathe.

Gently he turns her around. The tips of their noses are inches apart, breaths mingling in the moonlit darkness, his as rapid and shallow as her own. The knowledge that he's as nervous as she is comforts her.

"Need to kiss you," he says.

"Need to or want to?" she whispers.

"No difference when I'm lookin' in your eyes," he says.

When her mouth opens to say his name, he pulls her to him.

At first it's awkward and tentative. She's only ever kissed one boy, and now she has a terrible moment of wondering if this is really what everyone else has been talking about, this fumbling of lips and tongue tips and trying not to breathe right at the wrong time.

Then Caleb takes her chin in one hand, cups the side of her face in the other, centering them both.

His tongue slips between her lips. She relaxes, invites him in. Heat spreads from her scalp to the tips of her toes. Heat and a sense of having been suddenly connected to a man for the first time. Not just any man. Caleb. Strong, handsome, sure-to-be-a-giant-someday Caleb.

A phone rings in the distance.

They both ignore it

More rings. They stop.

Her father's high, barking cry pierces the night.

She wants to yank back from Caleb's kiss, but her mind fights with her desire. If Caleb is experiencing a similar struggle, she can't sense it. His kisses intensify, his arms around her now, gathering her T-shirt into his fists.

The house's sliding door squeals in its track. Her father's boots pound the cedar steps. Have they been caught?

"Caleb?" her father shouts. "Caleb? You out there, boy?"

She hears not anger but fear and sadness in her father's voice. He can't see them through the shadows.

"Yes, Mister Abel! I'm here."

"Come on up, son," her father says. "Something's happened…"

His face is hidden in the shadows, but his voice cracks with emotion.

"Sir?"

"It's your parents, Caleb. Something's happened to your parents."

1

Even though she's spent the past few days crying at work, Amber Watson Claire has managed to avoid shedding a single tear in front of her boss. So far her breakdowns have all started the same way. She loses herself in some menial task for about fifteen minutes, then she suddenly, violently remembers it's been less than a week since she opened the door to the storeroom at Watson's, the bar her father built, and found her husband plowing one of his bartenders with the abandon of a porn star.

The tangle of their sweaty, clawing limbs amidst cases of beer and piles of flattened cardboard boxes is like a frame of film she can't excise from the reel no mater how many times she pulls it from the projector and goes after it with a pair of scissors.

She sees them screwing when she's sorting her boss's mail into three neat piles—bills, junk, and personal.

She sees them screwing when she's printing out the seating chart for the Women of Industry breakfast at the Prestonwood Country Club her boss is scheduled to host later that month.

Everywhere Amber looks she sees the crazed rutting of her husband and that vile home wrecker in those last few seconds before the woman saw her standing in the doorway and let out a small scream.

She's not sure why, but she's convinced that after one week from that horrible, life-changing moment, things will get better. Or at least easier, if not altogether easy.

One week! That's all she needs.

One week between the present and those horrible twenty minutes it took her husband to empty his side of the closet into some suitcases, shouting excuses for his cheating while she sobbed in the other room.

Couldn't she see it was all her fault? She was the one who was always riding his ass. About what exactly he didn't say; maybe she'd said *Please don't break our marriage vows* one too many times for his liking? She was the cold fish in bed. She was the one who never wanted to be touched. The first accusation had been a steaming crock of bullshit, the second and third, outrages on par with his cheating.

For months she'd quizzed her girlfriends on how to liven things up between the sheets. And she hadn't just come up with new ideas. She'd bought toys, ordered costumes, printed dirty stories off the Internet she thought he would like and offered to read them to him. But every time she'd made an attempt to warm the chill that had gripped their bedroom for a year, he'd dismissed her like she was some sex freak. *The only problem, Amber, is that you keep saying there's a problem,* he'd told her again and again and again.

And yet, the one who couldn't connect was him, it turned out, and he couldn't connect because he was plugging himself into another socket every day at work.

"*Amber?*"

Her boss's confident baritone ripping out of the house's intercom system never fails to make her jump. But a few weeks into the job, she had trained herself not to scream whenever it happened. When she cries out this time, it leaves her red-faced and ashamed.

A short silence follows. Her boss heard her little outburst. Great.

"Darling, can I see you in my office upstairs?" Belinda Baxter says. Her East Texas twang makes everything she says sound vaguely accusatory, even when she throws in a *darling*, a *honey*, or a *sweetheart*.

"Be right there," Amber croaks, clearing her throat.

"Great. But first, honey, can you go to the wet bar in the living room and fix a vodka martini? I think Henry moved all the liquor in from the pool house after the Neighborhood Council meeting."

"How many olives?" Amber asks.

"However many you'd like, sweetheart. The drink's for you, not for me. See you in a bit."

So much for hiding my tears, she thinks.

She doesn't even like vodka, but when your wealthy boss offers you a top-shelf cocktail in the middle of a workday, you don't say no. That's just a given, she's sure of it. Maybe it's even written somewhere in the handbook of personal assistants. If there is a handbook for personal assistants. So far she's learned everything about working for Belinda on the fly, and she's only made a few missteps here and there. That's to be expected when you get hired to organize the personal details of a multimillionaire's life not on the basis of your actual resume, but because you made a moving speech about your late father's efforts to combat PTSD at a fundraiser organized by said multimillionaire.

The job comes with plenty of stress, but she can't think of a more comforting work environment, a sprawling, contemporary mansion in one of the best neighborhoods in Dallas. Indeed, Belinda's home is so thoroughly covered in cream-colored carpet and upholstery, so thoroughly dotted with fragrant room diffusers, sometimes she feels like she works inside of a really expensive breath mint no one can bring themselves to take a bite out of.

And Belinda's office would put Oprah's to shame. A fifteen-foot ceiling complete with a chandelier that would barely fit in Amber's living room. Soaring bookshelves in between gold- framed maps of all the oil fields her family has managed in the sixty years since her great grandfather struck black gold on his cattle ranch outside Fort Worth.

As usual, Belinda sits amidst this splendor dressed like she just stumbled out of a spin class. A pink workout visor sits on her tight cap of steel gray curls. Her yoga pants slide down her legs as she rests her sandaled feet on the edge of her antique black and gold Louis XIV desk.

Belinda doesn't look up when she enters, just keeps flipping through a copy of *Texas Monthly* so fast it looks like she's afraid all the pages will stick together if she pauses to read any of them. She loves her boss's mix of big money and no bullshit. Hell, she even invented her own term for it—*brash casual*. When Belinda took a liking to the phrase the minute she heard it, Amber knew they'd have a good relationship. Maybe even a kind of friendship.

"How's that drink, honey?" Belinda asks without looking up from her magazine.

"Haven't tried it yet. I'm no bartender."

"Have a seat and take a sip." She drops her feet to the floor and sets the magazine to one side.

Seated, Amber says, "I've got the seating chart for the Women of Industry breakfast all printed out if you—"

"Yeah, yeah, later. Sip, honey. That's an order."

As she feels the burn, she fights the urge to take in a deep, gasping breath and loses.

"Good stuff, huh?" Belinda asks.

"I'm not much of a drinker."

"I can tell."

"Am I getting fired?"

"You think I waste good vodka on people I'm about to fire?"

"It doesn't seem like your style, no."

"I figured if you had a drink in you, you'd be more likely to tell me the truth when I asked you what was really going on at home."

"I've told you the truth. We're having problems."

"Like *he left dirty dishes in the sink* problems or *her name's Tiffany and she makes him feel like a real man 'cause she's too young and stupid to know what a real man is* problems."

"Her name's Mary and she's twenty-four."

"Son of a bitch!" Belinda hurls the copy of *Texas Monthly* to the floor. "*Scum!* I knew he was scum. You gonna get offended if I tell you I knew your husband was scum? Knew it since he walked through the front door at my damn Christmas party."

"Just please don't tell me he hit on one of your nieces."

"Oh, hell, no. He didn't need to. I just had to look at him. That's all."

"Look at him?"

"I know his type. Five years ago he was God's gift to women. Now he's over thirty and the chicken fried steak's leaving its mark and the music career ain't happening, so he's expecting the world to make him feel as good as it did when no one was judging him on the content of his character. That's all Little Miss Mary's about."

Amber downs half the martini. This time it doesn't burn so much.

"There you go, sweetie," Belinda says.

"Wait…his *music career?* When did Joel tell you about his music career?"

"Wouldn't shut up about it at my Christmas party, soon as you were out of earshot. Forgive me for saying so but it didn't take a detective to figure out that the main reason he talked your daddy into leaving him that bar is so he'd have a stage for him and his band to play on. What the hell are they called again? The Junky Toadstools?"

"The Blinking Jailbirds." Just saying the name of her husband's band now feels like coughing up a razorblade.

Hell, just saying the name of her husband feels like coughing up a razorblade.

"God, that's worse. They any good?"

"No," Amber answers truthfully for the first time in her entire life.

"Well, there's one small blessing in all of this. You won't have to listen to them murder cats anymore."

"It's not that easy. The situation with the bar is...complicated."

"Yeah. How's he been at actually running the bar?"

"Not so great."

"Maybe that'll work in your favor. One thing's for sure. *I'll* work in your favor if you need it."

"Thank you, Belinda," Amber whispers. She's afraid if she answers in a full voice, her gratitude over this offer of assistance will cause her to break down again.

"Finish your drink, darlin'."

She complies, then gulps much needed air. "Listen, Belinda, if I've been falling down on the job, I apologize. I just need a week to—"

"You haven't been falling down on the job. Don't be so damn hard on yourself. I just got sick of listening to you cry. That's all."

"Wait. When did... Oh my God, were you listening to me cry on the intercom?"

"Honestly, I was hoping to overhear a phone conversation, but you're really good about not doing cell phone calls at work."

It's called texting, Amber thinks.

"I'm a bigger fan of Cowboys games, to be frank, but I had to know what was troubling my precious personal assistant on whom I rely for pretty much everything in the world now... Oh, don't get all sad faced on me. I only did it about five or six times."

"It's your house."

"Answer a question for me," Belinda says.

"Okay."

"Are you sad or are you just angry?"

"Can't I be both?"

"Nope."

"Why not?"

"You're one more than you are the other. That's always how it goes when marriages end. Pick one. Just for the sake of this discussion."

"Well, I cry all day at work, so what do you think?"

"What do you do when you're home?" Belinda asks, sinking back in her chair, hands clasped against her stomach.

"Not much."

"Liar," Belinda says with a smile.

"I've got a dartboard. I put his picture on it. It sounds stupid, but it makes me feel better."

"You any good at darts?"

"I've gotten better."

"Congratulations."

"Thanks, but there are easier ways to become a better darts player."

"I'm sure," Belinda says with a grunt. She leans forward suddenly. The chair rolls forward a few inches, the ends of its arms thudding against the edge of the desk. But Belinda's a small enough woman that she's still got plenty of room in which to make dramatic hand gestures. "You're not crying over what you've lost, Amber. You're crying because you don't know what lies ahead. That's a big difference."

"I take it you have some experience with this?"

"Three experiences to be exact. The first one cheated. The second one drank until I threw him out. The third once starved me in the bedroom 'cause he was hoping *I'd* cheat and then he could try to get some of my money."

"I see," she says.

"I didn't cheat, by the way."

"I didn't ask," Amber says. "None of my business."

"Oh, enough of that now. We're gonna get *all* up in each other's business today, girl."

Amber flushes.

"Oh, no! Not like that, Amber. I haven't swum in the lady pond since college. Don't get me wrong. I've got plenty of friends who do, but… We're having a heart to heart. That's all I'm saying."

"So this is your *heart* that you're showing me today?"

"You thought otherwise?"

Amber just stares at her.

"Fine!" Belinda cries, shooting up from the chair. "I'm telling you how you feel! And I'm doing it because I'm older and wiser and more experienced than you are. There. You happy?"

"Happy isn't really a word I'd apply to my situation just now."

"Well, waste as much time on tears as you want, Amber. But I saw y'all together. There was about as much love between you two as a rattler and my front tires."

"Which one am I? The snake or your Bentley?"

Belinda laughs.

She leans against a bookshelf, studying Amber with an expression Amber can only describe as serious. In another moment, the arch grin is gone and replaced by a look that seems both intent and faraway. Belinda's mind had traveled to another place. She's wondering if she should take Amber there with her.

"I know it hurts like hell," her boss finally says. "You married that man because he was handsome and charming and full of big promises. But when it came down to it, he wasn't very much at all."

"I didn't need him to become some big country music star."

"Of course not. You needed him to be a good husband, and he couldn't even do that *before* he cheated. It's hard to say, so I'll say it for you. Nod if you know it's true. You'll have to admit it someday."

Amber nods.

It makes her head feel heavy and her neck feel like it's got a spike in it, but she nods because it's the truth and Belinda's right; nodding is easier than saying it out loud. And now, for the first time since her marriage ended, she's crying in front of her boss. There's no denying it. Joel has been a man of broken promises for their entire marriage, he was just good at distracting her from the last broken promise by making a new and even bigger promise over the pricey champagne he'd bought her as an amends. This time, however, champagne's not going to fix a damn thing.

"It may not seem like it, but this is your moment, Amber." Her hands come to rest on Amber's shoulders. "This is your moment to decide what you really want, who you really are. The thing about you, girl, is you give all of yourself to people. It's just your nature. Personally I love it because it makes you a great assistant, but it's not about me right now. It's about you. And this is about the fact that whether you believe it or not, you're in a much better place than you think you are."

"How's that?" Amber croaks.

"You thought Joel was just second-rate and he ended up being last place. So it's not like you tried for the brass ring and fell flat on your face. Hell, you don't even know what kind of ring you want yet. Gold, silver, brass? It's up to you, babe. They're all yours to try for. Yours to discover. And *I* am gonna send you someplace that will make the whole discovery process easier."

"Like a spa day?"

Belinda cackles. "Oh, honey. It's a lot more than a spa day."

"Rehab for divorced people?"

"Nope. You got any plans in the next few weeks?"

"You mean aside from making sure my hu—*Joel* doesn't get the bar?"

"Two days. That's how much you'll need. Two days to get away. I'll give you the time off soon as we get your…appointment set up." Belinda hesitates over these last three words, as if everyday business terms don't apply to whatever she's talking about without really talking about it.

"No offense, Belinda, but I'm not really a seminar person."

"It's not a seminar. It changed my life for the better, but it's not a seminar."

"Well…what is it?"

Amber's startled by the seriousness in Belinda's expression.

"It's an experience," she whispers. "And by the time it's over, you'll have a much better grasp on who you really are. On who you really want."

"This *experience*…does it have a name?"

"The Desire Exchange," her boss answers.

"A sex club?" she cries before she can measure her tone. "You're sending me to a sex club?"

"It's far more than that."

"How much more?"

"A million flat. That's the price of admission. Which I'm gonna cover for you along with any other expenses related to the trip."

"I don't understand," she says because *thank you* seems premature.

Sure, it's a lot of money, but what the hell is it *for?*

"And you won't until you're there. But I promise you, I swear on every penny I have, *no one* will hurt you and you won't be forced to do anything you don't want to do."

"And you can't tell me anything else?"

"Except for this. When you leave The Desire Exchange, you'll leave behind a version of yourself that's caused you nothing but confusion and pain. The same version of yourself that thought Joel Claire was a great catch."

Belinda's one of the chattiest and most gossipy people Amber has ever met. But on the subject of this Desire Exchange place, her typical wisecracks have been replaced by the kind of proclamations Amber would expect to hear out of a lawyer or a judge. Maybe it's the hefty price tag involved. If there's one thing her boss takes seriously, it's money. And maybe for that reason alone, Amber should just get over it and say yes, despite the fact that she'd have absolutely no idea what she was agreeing to.

But she drank the martini when Belinda asked her, why not just—

Because it's a sex club! a voice that sounds like her mother's cries. *There's a big difference between a sex club and a martini! Especially when the price of admission is four times the cost of her house.*

"I can tell you this, sweetheart," Belinda says, sounding nothing like Amber's mother. "This isn't about letting off steam or making up for lost time or getting your inner wild child out of your system. It's more than that. So much more than that."

The expression on her boss's face does it. The satisfied, glassy-eyed smile. Whatever this Desire Exchange is, it took a woman like Belinda, a woman who's been given every blessing one could ask for, and gave her something more, something better.

Why not give it a try?

Amber's been a good little girl most of her life. Barely any hookups in college; none sober, anyway. Always waiting for date three before she gave anything away. And what did she get for all that? Manipulated, lied to, and cheated on.

"Fine," she hears herself whisper.

Just one word, but it feels like total surrender.

"Excellent!" Belinda cries, back to her chipper, hands-clapping self. "Now I'll just—"

The first text tone startles them both. It's Amber's phone. She waves her hand in the air to keep Belinda talking. But then there's another and another and another, and by the time Amber stands up and slides her phone from her pocket, she's got four messages in all. Two from Julio, the manager at Watson's, and two from Annabelle, who oversees the kitchen.

They all say the same thing.

"What is it?" Belinda asks.

"It's my hus—Joel," she says. "It's Joel. He's trying to change the locks at the bar."

"Go," Belinda cries. "Go now!"

Amber's already flying down the stairs by the time Belinda shouts, "Call me if you need help!"

2

For its first three years of operation, Abel Watson's struggling country music bar occupied a single storefront between an ice cream parlor and a yarn store in a lonely strip mall. Amber was just a toddler then. Later, her dad would tell stories about how his bacon was saved when a nearby subdivision announced a massive expansion, and shortly thereafter, he found himself the owner of an upscale alternative to the Ft. Worth Stockyards, a place for wealthy Dallasites to line dance and listen to authentic country music without first spending forty minutes in the car.

Today, Watson's takes up three storefronts instead of one. The once dreary strip small is now a bustling shopping center studded with elegant restaurants, a ladies only gym, and a condo high-rise. The mall's wealthy patrons clearly aren't used to seeing physical confrontations outside of places like The Big Bend Bread Factory and Muriel's French Kitchen. That must be why several of them are frozen in place, a few paces from their parked cars, gawking at the standoff between Watson's entire lunchtime staff and Amber's husband.

The van for some locksmith company is parked a few yards away, right next to Joel's dusty pickup.

Dressed for work in his Western duds, Julio, Watson's manager of ten years, stands right in front of the entry door. He's about half the size of Amber's soon-to-be ex-husband, but his arms are splayed across the door behind him, his body tense and taut, as if he's prepared to launch himself at Joel the second the man gestures for the locksmith to step out of his van.

Annabelle, the kitchen manager who used to babysit Amber when she was a little girl, is right next to him, still in her apron, her back pressed to one quarter of the entrance, arms crossed tightly over her boat's prow of a chest. She's wearing her apron which means she was in the middle of work when Joel started whatever this nonsense is.

"Profanity's not going to be your best choice, here, alright Julio?" Joel is saying when she walks up. "Now if you'd all just step aside, we can avoid involving law enforcement. And that, my folks, means we can also avoid checking on the immigration status of any—"

"We're all legal!" Julio shouts. "And you'd know that if you weren't a lousy manager."

"Why's that, Julio?" Joel asks.

Annabelle says, "You have our papers on file, asshole!"

"Alright, so apparently the cursing just isn't going to stop which means I'm gonna have to put in a call to our friends at the Dallas Po—" He's in mid-dial when he sees her charging toward him down the sidewalk. "Goddammit to hell!" he shouts at the crowd. "Now who called Amber? That is just *not* appropriate! That is not appropriate at all."

"What are you doing?" she asks.

It's the closest they've been in days. Everyone on the curb seems to know it. They're being stared at like strippers outside a church on a Sunday.

"We're gonna need to have a pause while we work all this out," Joel says quietly. "That's all."

"A *pause*. What the hell does that mean?"

"He's not just changing the locks, Amber," Julio shouts. "He's shutting the place down."

Annabelle says, "He came in 'bout a half hour ago and told us all to go home. Locksmith pulled up about five minutes after that and he got all pissed because the guy was early. He wanted us all gone so we wouldn't know he was try—"

"For the last time! I am *not* shutting the place down," Joel barks. "I am stopping business temporarily while we sort everything out. That's all."

"That's *all*? You've got four acts booked this week alone," she says. "What are you going to tell their managers?"

"That the club's working out some issues related to ownership and we'll rebook as soon as they've been sorted out."

"Related to ownership?" she screams.

"It's just a business term, Amber."

"*Ownership*? Of my *father's* bar?"

"We're gonna figure this out. Would you just relax already?"

"Three of those shows you're canceling are sold out, Joel! That doesn't sound like good ownership to me."

"Yeah, well, I changed our refund policy."

"You can't—Watson's has been in business for *twenty-five* years. You don't have the right to shut this place down on a whim."

"A whim, huh? Is that what you call the end of our marriage?"

Discussing the end of her marriage right now in front of everyone would be an indignity worse than what he put her through a few days before.

"This club isn't about *us*, Joel. It's about the people who work here. It's about the music. It's about my father. He trusted you to—"

"To run it, exactly. And this is me running it. I own Watson's so I'll—"

"An LLC owns Watson's!"

"Yeah, and I'm the majority partner. Because that's how your father wanted it. Because he knew you and your mother didn't know a damn thing about how to run a business."

"My father gave you this place because you bullied him into it on his deathbed!"

It's the first time she's ever spoken this truth out loud. And she expects it to knock her soon-to-be ex-husband off his feet.

But Joel Claire, it turns out, is nothing if not resourceful.

"There!" he cries. "Did everyone hear my wife's acknowledgment that her father *gave* me this bar?"

"I heard her!"

The shrill cry has come from the direction of Joel's truck. Mary, the same woman she caught her husband fucking a few days ago, throws herself halfway out of the passenger side window of his pickup truck, wearing a big smile on her rosy-cheeked face.

In a low voice, Annabelle says, "Dogs should keep their heads inside cars. They might get hurt."

"I heard that too," Mary cries.

"Oh, yeah? Bowwow, *puta!*" Annabelle shouts back.

"You're fired!" Joel shouts at Annabelle.

"Uh huh, sure," Annabelle responds without moving an inch.

"Stop it, Joel," Amber says. "Whatever you're doing, just stop it!"

"I am, Amber," Joel whispers. "I'm putting a stop to everything until we figure out what we're gonna do."

"We're getting divorced," she whispers back. "That's what we're gonna *do.*"

"I'm aware of that, sweetheart. I'm talking about the next verse of *my* song, not yours."

No thought to the years they've spent together. No thought for the plans they'd made for kids, for a life. Just a few days out from being caught red-handed with another woman and already her husband's thinking of the business, of money, of himself. She'd always made allowances for his ambition, had figured ambition was part of any exceptional man. But her husband, she can see now, isn't just ambitious; he's self-obsessed and greedy. The sight of him now, plotting his next career move with her father's life's work gripped in one fist, is a harder slap in the face than the sight of him fucking another woman.

"Jesus, Amber," Joel whispers at the sight of her tears. "Don't cry in front of them."

"Howdy, songbirds!" a familiar voice says from several feet behind her.

Amber hasn't laid eyes on him in four years, and even though she wouldn't have thought it possible, during that time Caleb has somehow grown taller and broader. He still walks with a casual, confident gait she'd be able to spot across a crowded arena, like he knows his sheer size is a better indication of his strength than any menacing pose could ever be. His Stetson's the right size now, unlike the ones he used to wear as a kid, and the brim shades the hard, etched features of a fully grown man, a man with a voice so deep it sounds like it's coming from some otherworldly place where he rules as king. His eyes are still so sparkling and blue she can't look into them without blushing. His jeans are scuffed and tattered, but his cowboy boots are brand new; so is his red and black plaid shirt. Not just new, spotless and freshly ironed.

Did he dress up a little for this surprise visit? Did he dress up for *her*?

"What are you doing here, Caleb?" Joel asks, his tone suddenly tense.

"Just got back in town last night. Thought I'd stop by the family business and have some lunch. But it doesn't look like lunch is being served."

"Who called him?" Joel shouts over one shoulder with real fear in his voice. No one answers. *"Who called him?"*

"Nobody called me, songbird," Caleb says. "Quiet down. You don't want to damage your signing voice there. Hey. You alright, Amber?"

"I…"

Her throat closes up. Maybe it's the shock of seeing Caleb for the first time in years. Maybe she just can't bring herself to spill her guts right there on the sidewalk, to paint the full picture of how awful Joel is being to her, to all of them.

"You know, well, uhm…" Joel says, with the nervous stutter of an elementary school student giving his first presentation in front of his classmates. "I'm sorry to say I've got to close the place for a week or two." Joel's voice seems to get a little shakier with each step Caleb takes toward him. "I'm not sure if you've heard but Amber and I…Well, we've decided to end our marriage."

Caleb freezes, expression hard as stone and impossible to read.

"I hadn't heard that, no."

There's now about three feet of space between Joel and the man she cannot bring herself to call her brother despite what the adoption papers might say.

"Well…" Joel says. "In light of that—I mean, given how much there's going to be to deal with, we just need to stop operating for a short while and then we'll be back—"

"How long's a while?" Caleb asks.

"Just a few weeks 'til we gets things sorted out. Now, with all due respect, this is a family matter so if you could ju—"

"I am family," Caleb says.

"On paper, maybe. But come on, now. We all know Abel was just—"

"My father," Caleb says. "Abel Watson was the only real father I ever had."

"Sure, sure. Of course. But if you'd ju—"

"He cheated on her, Caleb!" Annabelle snaps. "She caught him in the back room last week with that girl over there in his truck. Now he's trying to take the bar so he can use it to promote his crappy band."

"*Shut up, Annabelle!*" Joel cries.

Caleb's entire body goes rigid. Amber's seen this change overtake him many times, mostly when they were teenagers and brawling became Caleb's preferred method for dealing with his grief for his parents. She knows just where to look for the telltale sign of the anger knotting itself through his soul; it's in the right corner of his powerful jaw. The tension there is suddenly so strong it sends that section of his jawbone into sharp relief. He has to tilt his head gently to one side to be rid of it, an oddly prim gesture for a guy on the verge of venting rage.

"That true, Amber?" Caleb asks.

"Yes. I caught 'em. It's true."

Joel takes a step toward Caleb. "Look, I don't mean to be blunt, *cowboy*, but this doesn't concern you, alright? And Amber and I don't need to litigate our marriage right here in front of—"

The punch is so silent and swift Amber's not sure where it landed. One minute Joel's standing, the next he's flat on his back. No blood comes from his nostrils. The hand Joel finally manages to bring to his face lands weakly on his jaw. As he wheezes, he blinks up at Caleb as if he's in genuine fear for his life.

"Try to get up," Caleb says quietly. "Just fucking try it. I dare you."

Joel doesn't get up.

Caleb steps off the sidewalk and starts for Joel's pickup truck.

"Drive away!" he calls to the terrified woman in the passenger seat.

"*What?*" Mary squeals. In her panic, she's pulled off one of her shoes and she's holding it beside her head like a makeshift baton.

"Roll up the window and drive away," Caleb says firmly.

"It's *his* truck!" Mary whines.

"Don't care," Caleb answers.

"Where am I supposed to go?" Mary asks.

"Somewhere Amber doesn't have to look at you. You got all of North Texas to choose from. Take your pick and get moving."

Mary crawls over the gearshift and into the driver's seat. Without taking her eyes off Caleb, she starts rolling up the window like a swarm of killer bees are heading straight for Joel's pickup. Caleb points at the parking lot's nearest exit.

The tires literally squeal as Joel's mistress abandons him.

As if he's just completed a task as simple as removing a kink from a garden house, Caleb turns and walks back toward the spot where Joel is still flat on his back, rubbing his bruised jaw with one hand.

"Got any brain damage there, songbird?" Caleb asks.

Joel wheezes.

"Okay. Good. 'Cause I'm gonna need you to take this all in, and it's complicated, so pay attention. You know that trust fund Abel set up to provide you with a cushion while you got started? The one that's got the proceeds of his retirement in it? The one you've been relying on for your marketing budget now for *four years*? Guess who's the trustee?"

Joel groans.

"Yeah, see, he didn't want to make me a partner in the LLC 'cause he didn't want you to think he didn't trust you. But just in case you *did* turn out to be a steaming stack of shit on a hot highway, he wanted a fail-safe in place. And that fail-safe's me, asshole."

"Whu—what do you…?" Joel tries.

"It means you do anything other than make a graceful exit—and by graceful, I mean you sign over your majority share back to Amber *tomorrow*—then your little slush fund's gone." Caleb snaps his fingers to indicate how quickly he'll make that happen. "And in your case, that means no radio spots, no T.V. spots, no nothing to promote any band you'd even think about bringing in here. Including *yours.* The Shitty Taillights, or whatever the hell they're called."

"The Blinking Jailbirds," Joel mutters in a lisping voice. That's when Amber notices his bottom lip is swelling. "You can't…You can't do that. You—"

"I can and I will," Caleb says. "Four years now and you've got this place down to just above the red. Every other week you're switching out a menu item to something three times the cost. Paying shit-ass consultants thousands to find out what it would take to turn the place into a *wine bar.* You know damn well if you have to run this place off what you make from buffalo steaks and Corona, there won't be a dollar left to launch your music career. So sure, songbird. Go right ahead. Make a play. And I'll make sure you won't get a single band, manager, agent, or A&R guy anywhere within a hundred feet of you and this place."

She's more startled by the facts Caleb's just revealed in his speech than she was by the sight of her husband cheating on her.

Caleb, a *trustee?*

She's barely heard from him in four years, ever since her father died. Just a postcard here and there, usually with a line or two about whatever job he'd managed to land that month. Truck driver in the North Dakota oil fields. Ranch hand at some big spread up in Montana.

She figured he'd taken her father's death—*their* father, she reminds herself, against her will—harder than she had. She'd never imagined him playing any role at all in the business, not now, not ever. And yet, the whole time he'd been gone, the whole time he'd been riding the ranges, driving oil-filled trucks through the lonely highways of the Great Plains, Caleb had been reviewing paperwork and bank documents, using his position as trustee to monitor Joel's stewardship of her father's lifework.

Of course, he couldn't have learned all of what he'd just said from the bank. He'd probably stayed in touch with Julio and Annabelle too. The knowledge that for the past few years Caleb has been closer than she realized leaves her breathless. She's not sure if she likes the feeling.

Things seemed easier when Caleb was far away. For her heart, at least. For her head. But given how bad things are now, apparently it only seemed that way. In fact, now that he's back, it looks like things are going to get a lot better.

Joel struggles to his feet. The bruise on the left side of his jaw has doubled in size. When he goes to speak, his swollen lip seems to cause him so much sudden pain his sneer turns into a pained grimace.

"I don't need this place," he finally manages. "I don't need...*you two!*" He says the last words with such venom she's surprised when he doesn't follow them up by spitting at her feet. "You can have it. Take it. Run it *together.* Make it your special little project. I'm sure y'all will have a blast. Brother and sister, sitting in a tree—"

"Joel," she says before she can stop herself.

"Oh, come on. I've seen the way you look at him—"

"Joel," Caleb says this time. "There may be a saying about not punching the same man twice in one day, but I ain't ever heard it."

Joel gives them both a leering grin. When he starts to walk away, his first steps become stumbles.

Caleb moves out of his path, hands out and a polite smile on his face, like someone letting a drunk move past them in a crowded bar. Amber can hear sighs of relief from the staff when Joel gets a few yards from the curb and yanks his phone from his jeans pocket. But just then, he spins in place. She's surprised when he shouts a name other than her own.

"Hey, Annabelle," he shouts. "Since I finally got the chance to say this, your food? It's *shit!*"

"Oh, Mister Joel," Annabelle says with a broad grin. "That's 'cause I always added something special just for you."

Joel does his best impression of an idiot's laugh. But Annabelle keeps smiling and nodding, as if the memory of whatever she added to Joel's meals is a warm and happy thing that will sustain her for years to come.

His parting shot having missed its target, Joel stumbles off into the parking lot.

"So," Caleb says, "who wants some lunch?"

3

Watson's is so cavernous it feels to Amber like she and Caleb are the only ones inside. But Annabelle and her three cooks are busy making up for lost time in the kitchen while Julio and his servers frantically set up tables on the three levels of platforms surrounding the empty, sunken dance floor.

Nothing bums her out more than the sight of a dark stage, but apparently she's in the minority, because in a few minutes, the place will be packed with hungry regulars even though the only music will be coming from the jukebox.

Caleb walks up to the beer taps like he owns the place which, given what she learned a few moments before , he just might. He fills a pint glass with amber ale and sets it on the bar in front of her with a loud *thunk*.

"Thanks," she says. "But I had a martini at work."

"Hot damn!" he says. "I want your job."

"Not enough manual labor for you," she says. "And since when do you like martinis?"

"Since never. 'Sides, looks like I'm out of the job market now."

"How's that?"

"Gonna have my work cut out for me with this place."

"You're staying?" she asks.

Does this excite her or fill her with dread? She always feels a mixture of both when Caleb's around.

"Somebody's gotta run this place now that Joel's out of the picture."

"Caleb, I really appreciate what you did out there. Seriously, I do. But I'm not sure it was enough to get Joel out of the picture for good."

"You're not asking me to kill him, are you? Can I pat you down? You wearing a wire?"

"No!" she barks.

"No to which? The wire or the pat down?"

"I don't think Joel is through with us yet, is what I'm saying."

"Fine. Next time I'll aim for his stomach." He sinks his teeth into his lower lip, throws a mock punch into the air in front of him.

"Be serious. Please."

"Oh, I'm damn serious. He's not getting his hands on anything in this bar. Not the jukebox. Not the barstools. Not *nothing*. And I'm sticking around to make sure of it. Unless, you know, you think you can handle this place by yourself."

"I didn't say I didn't want you around."

"Didn't say you said that, sis."

"Please don't call me that!"

The words slip out before she can stop them, words she's stopped herself from saying again and again over the years whenever Caleb referred to her as his sister or called Abel his dad. They sound as dismissive and possessive as she feared they would. Like she's just some spoiled only child who doesn't want to share her father.

Explaining the far more complicated truth of the matter would fill her with shame. And besides, part of him *must* know.

Is that why he's staring at her now with the same intense gaze she used to dream about when they were teenagers?

He's certainly not doing that thing he usually does when he's hurt and trying to hide it; he doesn't cast his eyes to one side while he puckers his lips and looks for a task to distract himself with. Instead, he stares at her as if he's waiting for her to explain, waiting for her to take them back to the night on the boat dock before everything changed.

She can't look into those blue eyes for very long without the world feeling like it doesn't have an up or a down anymore. So she takes a sip of beer instead.

"I already called the bank while you were in the bathroom," he says. "No more automatic deposits into the operating fund. Not until we get this cleaned up. And I'm sorry to lay this on you this hard, Amber, but Joel won't give two shits about this place if there's nothing in that operating fund for him to spend on his band."

She doesn't need him to say the rest, that Joel doesn't care about *her* either. The only thing that makes this easier to accept is the dawning realization that Joel isn't really capable of caring about anyone except himself.

Good luck, Mary. Hope you used protection!

"So that's it?" she asks. "One call and the deposits stop?"

"They're not stopping. They're going into my checking account. I'll pay the bills myself until we kick Joel out of the LLC."

"You can do that? I mean, is that really how Dad set up the trust?"

"Yep," he answers.

"So this whole time you could have raided that trust fund with a phone call and instead you were driving trucks and working oil fields?"

"Not the whole time. A few years back I was a hand on a big spread outside Surrender, Montana. Didn't you get my postcards?"

Yeah, and who sends postcards anymore? she almost says. But she answers her own question instantly—*people who are afraid of e-mail because it gives them too much space to talk about forbidden feelings.*

"Still," she says.

"Abel trusted me to make the right call. The right call was giving you and Joel a shot. And giving you and Joel a shot meant giving Joel a shot at running this place. Also, it seemed like you loved him."

"You think I'm an idiot, don't you?" she says.

"I've never thought anything of the kind, Amber."

"You, Dad. You both knew. That's why you set up the trust like that. You both knew Joel was awful and you were just too afraid to say—"

"That's not true, Amber. We would've had doubts about anybody, *anybody* you were going to marry, especially someone who thought he was good enough to run the family business. If we'd had any idea what a shit Joel was going to turn out to be, we wouldn't have let him within ten feet of the house. Or you."

"I still feel like an idiot," she whispers.

"Well, that's a bunch of bull. You have to try for stuff, especially when it comes to marriage."

"Got a lot of experience in the marriage area, huh?"

Now Caleb does look away quickly.

When he turns his back to her and opens the nearest register, she realizes he's not hurt. He's hiding something.

"Wait a minute," she says. "Wait just a minute. You got *married?*"

She looks to the hands he's suddenly counting bills with. No ring.

"Did you really get married without telling us?" she asks.

"It was a spur of the moment thing."

"Like a Vegas spur of the moment thing?"

"No!"

"Are you still married?"

"*No!*"

"I can't believe you didn't tell me."

He shakes his head at the register, but he doesn't say anything.

She remembers the way he acted at her own wedding, how uncomfortable he looked inside the suit her father had bought for him just a few weeks before. He'd never been a big drinker, probably because of what alcohol had done to his father, but he'd shotgunned so many Coronas during the first twenty minutes of the reception, she'd been afraid he was going to embarrass himself. Instead, he ended up silent and sullen and rooted to a far corner of the reception hall where he ignored the flirtations of a dozen different women. Every few minutes, she'd caught him staring at her. And then there'd been his curt good-bye—a brief peck on the cheek for her, and for Joel, a hard clap on the back followed by the words, "You break her heart and I'll rip you to fucking shreds, dude." And then he was gone before either she or her new husband could remark that his parting words were the kind of thing an ex-boyfriend might say, not an adopted brother.

Maybe Caleb had wanted to spare her the same discomfort, the same storm of conflicted feelings, by not telling her about his spur of the moment wedding.

Maybe he was trying to spare her now by not giving her the details.

"I want details," Amber says.

"It was lonely work I was doing. She was transitioning away from someone else."

"You mean rebounding."

"Yeah. Sure. Rebounding. Whatever. We parted as friends. Maybe because we didn't have a bar to fight over."

"How'd you meet her?"

"I don't want to talk about her."

"Doesn't seem fair," she mumbles, sipping her beer.

"*What* doesn't seem fair?" he says, cocking one eyebrow and giving her a sidelong look while he counts bills.

"I don't know. Having the end of my whole marriage laid out on the sidewalk outside for you like road kill, and I just ask for a few details and suddenly you're like—"

"That is so like you, Amber."

"What? *What's* so like me?"

"That's what people call a false equivalency."

"False equivalency? That's not a Caleb expression. Where'd you learn that one? Your ex-wife? What was she? A college professor?"

"She was a scheduler I worked with up in North Dakota. They've barely got any pipeline up there so I was doing truck pickups from fracking platforms all day long. It started with radio talk and then moved on to dinner."

And then all those hard muscles of yours flexing as you bring yourself down onto the body of some strange woman and—

"And then marriage," she adds to distract herself from this image.

"Uh huh. But no baby carriage. And no white wedding I didn't invite you to either. So stop acting all butthurt and drink your beer. I'm here to save the day, remember?"

"Butthurt. Now *there's* a Caleb expression."

"Glad to see you haven't lost your mouth, sis," he says.

Done counting the money, he bumps the register drawer shut with one hip.

This time she doesn't ask him not to call her sis again. But she can see the challenge in his eyes. Did he use the term again on purpose? Does he want her to snap at him again for using it so that he can finally, after all these years, come right out and ask her why she really hates it when he refers to her as his sister?

"So here we are," Caleb finally says. "Pushing thirty and both divorced. Abel Watson was a helluva man but he sure didn't teach us how to stay married, did he?"

She knows he's kidding, but his words cut deep. The cocky grins fades from his expression as soon as he sees the look on her face.

"Hey," he says quietly. "That— Shit, that came out wrong. Sorry."

"It's fine," she whispers.

Amber allowed herself a few minutes of tears after they all filed back into the bar. But she'd been in the bathroom alone. Not sitting at the bar in front of Caleb.

He's resting one hand on top of hers, so gently she almost didn't notice at first. She stares at it. Tells herself to look up into his eyes because his eyes will tell her what this sudden touch actually means. But she can't. She just stares at his powerful, veined hand, hears her next words as if some other version of her has spoken them.

"When a man won't sleep with his wife, that's a problem, right? I mean, she should know something's wrong... Right?"

He removes his hand so quickly, she's left to wonder if he thinks that touching her in any way when she simply mentions sex might seal them together in some awkward or painful way.

"Maybe," Caleb says.

His Adam's apple bobs. He sucks in a quick breath through his nose and grips the counter on either side of him.

"We don't usually talk about sex stuff," he finally says with a startling blend of tension and hunger in his voice, the same way he'd tell a woman she was wearing a pretty dress even though he was really thinking of what she'd look like once he'd pulled her out of it.

"It's a simple question, Caleb."

"You're asking the wrong one."

"Am I?"

"You're asking if it's your fault. You're asking if you should take on the burden of a man like Joel. The answer's no. Scratch that. The answer's *hell* no. Kick his ass to the curb and get the hell out. But don't take responsibility for his failings. Not now, not ever. Feelings aren't a choice. Cheating is. If he was half a man, he would have come to you about the stuff that was making him want to cheat six months before he ever did it. If he were a *real* man, he would have copped to the fact that the stuff that was making him want to cheat probably didn't have a damn thing to do with you."

For the first time in years, she allows herself to gaze into Caleb's eyes, those beautiful, dazzling blue eyes. Her *brother's* blue eyes. And for the first time in a while, this knowledge doesn't dim her fantasies of what it would be like to taste his lips again, to rock forward into his powerful embrace.

She allows her mind to swim in the memory of that long ago night before everything changed, when the two of them were brought together by the promise of becoming something altogether different than what they are today.

Caleb stares right back. Has he gone back to the boat dock of her father's lake house?

Is he remembering what it felt like to gather her T-shirt into his fists in those last blissful moments before her father's cry pierced the dark?

It's no matter. Her father's voice returns just as it always does in moments like these, with the exact same tone he'd used with her that one time they were hiking and he overturned a log with a snake coiled under it.

Back away, girl, he'd say. *Back away, right now.*

Caleb's had his moments of aggression over the years, but he's no snake.

Still, the ghost of her father stands between them now. Her father's wishes. Her father's plans.

Her phone vibrates on the bar in front of her.

It's a text from Belinda asking if she's okay.

"I need to get back to work," she says.

"Not sure you should be driving right now," Caleb says.

"I bet. You're the one who just served me a beer even though I told you I had a martini at work."

"Is that why you want to get back? Your boss has better well drinks?"

"My boss doesn't serve well drinks."

"I forget. She's a fancy lady."

"She's got a fancy house. She's practically a cowgirl at heart. Kinda like your ex-wife, it sounds like."

"Uh huh. Julio'll get someone to drive you. Or I could drive you."

Alone in the car with Caleb. The thought makes her head spin. Amazing how many times in her life she's avoided being alone with him for more than ten or fifteen minutes. The effort became so commonplace when they were younger that it took Caleb leaving town for her to realize how much it had exhausted her.

"Belinda's got a driver," she says too quickly, like she's trying to protect herself from the fact that Caleb is just being a good guy.

"Suit yourself," he says.

"Thank you. For everything."

"Sure thing," he says.

"I'd give you a hug, but…"

"I'm behind the bar. Right. Don't worry about it."

She picks up her phone in one hand and gives him a weak wave with the other. A few paces from the bar, she turns. He hasn't moved an inch. He's staring at her with one hand resting on the counter next to the register.

"Where are you staying?" she asks.

"Old friend's letting me crash with him for a while."

"Where?"

"Denton."

"*Denton*? That's far!"

"Yeah, well, looks like I'll be looking for a place closer in now. Closer to this place, anyway."

"Keep me posted," she says.

"Sure thing, sis."

She steps through the entrance. On the sidewalk, she sucks in a deep, hungry breath of humid air.

She's not drunk. But Caleb's right. She shouldn't drive. And she wonders now if the real reason he put that beer in front of her was because he didn't want her to leave at all.

Then

Standing on the tip of the dock, Amber watches Caleb race up the cedar steps toward her dad. They're about to smack into each other when her dad seizes Caleb by his shoulders, halting him mid-stride.

Maybe she was wrong about the sadness in her father's voice a few seconds before.

Maybe he really is about to whoop Caleb within an inch of his life for giving her a kiss that made her forget her name. But violence isn't her father's style. At least not when she's around. But it is her father's style to pull the Band-Aid off in one swift motion. That's why it takes him a few seconds to deliver the awful news.

After promising to stay sober thirty days, Caleb's father snuck out to his local watering hole where his mom found him on his favorite barstool and literally dragged him out into the parking lot. The tussle that ensued might have ended uneventfully in any other environment, but on the side of a busy freeway it sent them both into the path of an eighteen-wheeler, killing them instantly.

She has never seen her father deliver news this terrible before. She's got no sense of what he's going to do now that the words are out.

A wail of pure anguish rips from Caleb, filled with more pain than any fifteen-year-old should be allowed to feel. Her father throws his arms around the boy, so tightly it looks as if he's afraid the news will literally drive Caleb apart. In that moment, her love for her dad grows roots nothing will be able to dig up.

She joins them, holding up the right side of Caleb's suddenly boneless body while her father holds up the left. The three of them struggle up the steps as Caleb's sobs rend her soul. But a part of her knows the crying is good and healthy, even if the cause is horrible. Caleb's releasing all the pain and anger he's kept bottled up for years now, and Amber and her father are right there to help him through it.

"Get him to bed," her dad whispers as soon as they're inside.

In the guest room, Caleb collapses onto the mussed comforter, curls into a fetal position, and starts to cry harder when she curls up behind him and drapes one arm over his side. She keeps her own tears as quiet as possible. That only seems right.

In the living room her father makes a frantic-sounding series of phone calls. She can only make out every few words. He's booking flights, it sounds like, or maybe he's just breaking the news to people. She's not sure.

Because they're spooning, she doesn't see him reach up to where her hand is resting against his chest. Instead, she feels his fingers close around hers and she returns his grip.

She has no words for him as powerful as simply being there with him, beside him in the dark. When staying silent becomes too much for her, she gently kisses the back of his neck. He gives her fingers a little squeeze in response.

The house is silent. She's not sure how much time has passed.

Suddenly her dad's silhouette blocks the light from the hallway. With careful steps he moves into the darkened bedroom. He sets a glass of water on Caleb's nightstand, grips the boy's shoulder, studies him through the shadows.

"Making arrangements to get you home, son," her dad says. "I'm going to go with you, get you through everything you need to do, 'kay?"

"Yes, sir," Caleb croaks.

"I need Amber for a minute. You going to be okay in here for a few?"

"Yes, sir."

She follows her father downstairs to the living room.

On the muted television, Dave Letterman cracks a joke and a faraway audience of people laugh silently. The sight seems obscene given what's happening, so she looks away from it quickly as if it's burned her eyes.

In a hushed whisper, her father says, "My buddy Dale Parsons is at his place on the other side of the lake and he flew his Cessna up. He'll fly us back to Dallas."

She's not surprised that her father is all business in this moment. Her mother has explained it to her countless times—this is how her father loves people. He organizes; he manages. She figures he's avoiding eye contact because he doesn't want her to see that he's been crying.

"Okay," she whispers. "Should I get my things?"

"No, you're staying," he says quickly, as if this were an obvious fact she'd simply overlooked. "I know you hate being here alone so Miss Lita, Dale's wife, she's coming over to stay with you. You remember her, right? You met her at Fourth of July last year. Remember?"

"I remember," she says. But her own voice sounds far away suddenly. Something else is happening here, and she's not sure what. "Who's going to bring me back to Dallas?"

"I just spoke to your momma and she's going to cut her visit to her sister short and take Southwest in tomorrow. She'll probably be here by the afternoon. I'll leave the SUV up at the airport so y'all can drive it back to Dallas. No need for you to rush either. There's gonna be a lot he and I are going to have to deal with as soon as we get back. A whole helluvalot."

"Why can't I just go with y'all?"

"I don't think there's room on the plane."

She knows this isn't true. Dale Parsons flies his whole family up sometimes and they've got three kids. And her dad's choice of words is weird. *I don't think there's room.*

Why didn't he ask if there was room?

"Daddy..."

Suddenly her father grips her shoulders tightly. He's got an angry furrow to his brow. When he clears his throat, she realizes he's about to say words he's been practicing in his head for a few minutes now. "Amber, look. I know how you feel about the boy. I know what y'all were doing down there, but that needs to change now. You understand me? Caleb's gonna be in our lives now, but not in the way you want. And that's what's best for *him*. So you need to take all those feelings you're having for him and you need to change 'em. You need to turn 'em into something else. Something that's better for him. Do you understand me, girl? Are you hearing me right now?"

Better for him. Such simple words, and he said them in such a measured tone. But she's registered them the way she might register a slap to the face.

All her feelings for Caleb, all her dreams about him, all the longing looks she's given him that summer, her father could sense all of it. And he's judged her for it, judged her as bad. So bad, he thinks he has to put a stop to those feelings in the middle of this awful moment that will change their lives forever. He's determined to keep her and Caleb apart at the very moment when Caleb is most vulnerable.

She's always been a daddy's girl. The title's never bothered her in the slightest. Everyone agrees: her dad's a success in life and he's going to make her a success too. He's saved enough money for her to go to a good college. He's a war hero who will walk through fire for his fellow vets. Sure, he's controlling and overbearing, but the way he controls things, it all usually works out in the end. Right now, though, she wants to bat his hands from her shoulders. She wants to scream in frustration, and holding in that scream is making her jaw quiver. She can feel it.

"Amber," he says, an angry edge to his voice now. "Do you *hear* me?"

"Yes," she whispers. "I hear you, Daddy."

"Good," he whispers. Then he brings his hand to the side of her face, suddenly affectionate, suddenly relieved, like she's agreed to take medicine he's sure will save her life.

"I'm sorry, honey," he says. "I know it's not what you want. But it's like I always say, sometimes the road rises up to beat you instead of meet you." It's one of his favorite sayings, one he claims to have invented, and one he only uses when some grand plan of his has been defeated despite his best efforts. Saying it now has clearly sent regret coursing through him given how Mister Tim and Miss Abby were killed. "God in heaven," he whispers. "I'm gonna have to shelve that old saw after tonight."

A few seconds later, Miss Lita knocks on the glass door. When her father slides it open, she steps into the living room quietly, her eyes glassy from a combination of drowsiness and shock. It's clear she dressed in a hurry. Her thick ponytail is already coming free of its rubber band. When she sees the look on Amber's face, she curves an arm around her shoulders and steers her into the kitchen.

The neighbor's sudden tenderness frees the tears Amber's been fighting. She turns her back to the living room so her father won't see, but from the way the older woman is rubbing circles on her back, it's clear to all of them what Amber's doing.

"Where's Caleb?" Lita asks.

"In the guest bedroom," Amber whispers.

"Should we go sit with him?"

"No," Amber says, her voice a tremble. "No, we shouldn't."

4

Now

"Married?" Amber's mother says for the third time in three minutes.

"Yep," Amber answers.

She's been home for over an hour but she hasn't moved an inch from where she collapsed on the sofa right after stumbling through the front door. Reaching for the portable phone and dialing her mother's number took most of the energy she had left.

At some point, maybe a few hours from now, she'll get around to taking her shoes off. Maybe.

She can't remember a day in her life this exhausting that didn't involve moving or a six-hour plane flight or a spin class. But her mood has improved dramatically since lunchtime. That's for sure. Maybe it was coming home to discover Joel hadn't done anything shitty to the house. Maybe it's the familiar and comforting sound of her mother's voice.

Or maybe it's because Caleb's back...

"For how long?" her mother asks.

"Couldn't have been more than a year or two. He was only gone four and they're already divorced."

"Divorced or separated?"

"Not sure. He just said it was over. And there's no ring. I'm surprised he didn't tell you, at least."

"Oh, I'm not. He never had the kind of connection to me that he had to your dad."

"That's true, I guess."

"This business with Joel and the bar. You sure you don't want me to come?"

"God, why? So he can torture you too?"

"I'm serious, sweetheart. Say the word and I'll hop in the car."

Her mother was being charitable, to say the least. For her *a hop in the car* meant a drive of several hours, at least.

Her mom's life choices these past few years had given proof to her dad's old saying. *Try to make an ER nurse retire and she'll end up treating the sunset.*

Right after her husband's death, she'd been invited to spend some time in the Texas Hill Country by her old friend Amanda Crawford, a woman whose personal wealth rivaled Belinda's. Amanda's ten-room mansion perched on a hill just outside the town of Chapel Springs was the perfect vantage point from which to take in the surrounding paradise of rolling green hills, orchards, and rushing creeks terminating in swimming holes full of crystal-clear water.

The two women were as close as sisters, thanks to a fateful night fifteen years before when Amber's mom and some other nurses at Baylor Hospital saved the life of Amanda's husband after his ER visit landed him in the care of an idiot doctor who misdiagnosed his chest pains as a panic attack. Years later, Amanda's husband would succumb to the same heart condition Amber's mother had discovered that night, but if it hadn't been for her mother's quick thinking, Amanda would have had to bury her husband ten years too soon.

When her mother fell in love with Chapel Springs right off the bat, Amber wasn't the least bit surprised. But when she called a few days later to inform Amber she was moving there for good, Amber's jaw hit the floor.

Amanda Crawford's invite, it turned out, had been twofold.

The woman had just purchased an old ranch house she planned to transform into a luxury bed and breakfast and she'd invited the four nurses who had saved her husband's life that long ago night to join her in the endeavor. And all of them had accepted. Including Amber's mom. Never mind that The Haven Creek Inn wasn't due to open for another year and a half.

Four years later, Haven Creek, as locals called it, was considered one of the premiere travel destinations in all of Texas. And it comforts Amber to think of her mother there now, safe, serene, surrounded by both beautiful country and the wonderful group of women who helped walk her through her grief over her husband's death.

"Stay put, momma," Amber says. "I think I'm gonna be okay."

"Caleb's got everything under control?"

"Something like that. Did you know all that stuff about the trust?"

"I knew your father and Caleb had a lot of conversations about it and they didn't include me. Like I said, the connection between those two...it was special. I tried not to intrude."

"And Joel?"

"What do you mean?" her mother asks.

"Did you have any doubts about him?"

"Amber, you *have* to stop doing this to yourself."

"Doing what?"

"Beating yourself up like this. Marriage is a roll of the dice and you never know how it's going to come out."

"But you can't win if you don't play?"

"If you want to be sarcastic, that's fine, I guess."

"I figure I'm allowed."

"Maybe for another few weeks."

"Remember that expression Daddy used to always say?"

"Which one?"

"Sometimes the road rises up to beat you instead of meet you."

"Oh, yeah. He stopped saying it after what happened to Caleb's parents."

"He only reserved it for the big things too. Not the everyday stuff. The big plans that went off the rails."

"I remember."

"Like a marriage. Think he'd use it now?"

"Well, he stopped using it altogether after Tim and Abby were killed, so no, I don't think he would. And this sounds suspiciously like you beating yourself up again so I'm not going to sign off on it."

"What about this thing I do with the dartboard? I took Joel's picture and I—"

"You told me about that already. That's fine."

"Okay. Good. Also, my boss is kinda sending me to a sex club," Amber adds.

"Hold, please," her mother says quietly.

"Uh huh," Amber answers, steeling herself for what's to come.

Her mother places one hand over the phone's mouthpiece and politely asks whoever's in the office with her to leave. Amber hears chair legs scrape wood floor, then her mother says, "A *what?*"

"A sex club. But it costs a lot of money. So I'm sure it's real nice."

"Your boss, Belinda Baxter, who has twice been on the cover of

Texas Monthly, is sending you to a sex club?"

"I kinda had the same reaction when she said it."

"But you're going anyway."

"Yes…" At least, she thinks she is.

When Freddy, Belinda's driver, brought her home from Watson's earlier that day, Belinda had departed for a day full of lunch, fitness classes, shopping, probably a few stops off at some places that served fine wine in a comforting environment, and then some more shopping.

A note had been waiting for her on Belinda's desk. *Stick to the light list for the rest of the day*, it said, referring to the list of long-term household projects she was supposed to focus on in between managing Belinda's social calendar and travel schedule. *Will call you later tonight about TDE.*

"I figure it'll relax me," Amber says.

"A weekend out here at The Haven Creek Inn will relax you. We have two massage therapists now."

"It's probably not the same."

"Oh, I'm sure it's not the same, Amber. That's my point. If relaxation's what you're after, it can be achieved in other ways."

"Okay, fine! It's not just what I'm after."

"As long as you're admitting to it."

"Momma, it's been a year since that man kissed me on the mouth. I tried everything to get things going in the bedroom again. *Everything.* And he treated me like I was some kind of desperate, needy freak. And the whole time, he was—"

"I know, I know. You don't have to justify yourself to me, Amber."

"Well, I do if you're gonna get all judgy."

"I'm not being *judgy*. I'm just… This is a sensitive time for you, Amber, I just—I want you to be clear on what your motives are. Don't say you're just looking for a good time when in your heart you're looking for something else."

"Like *looooooooooove?*"

"Hello, fifteen-year-old Amber. Could you give the phone back to twenty-six-year-old Amber, please?"

"Oh, Momma. I appreciate what you're saying. I really do. But I have needs. And Belinda has never stayed at a hotel that doesn't have five stars, so that means whoever's gonna be tending to my needs at this place, they're gonna be *real* high end."

"Are you drunk?"

"Just a teensy bit."

"Is that why you're telling me all this stuff?" her mother asks.

"No. I'm going to be gone for a couple days coming up and I need someone to know where I'm going."

"Okay. When are you going?"

"I don't know yet."

"Okay... Where is this place?"

"I don't know that yet either."

"Well, alrighty then," her mother says with a sigh. "This has been very informative, Amber. Thank you."

"But when I do know, I'll tell you."

"And tell Caleb."

"Are you crazy? I'm not telling *Caleb* about any of this!"

"Why not? If something goes wrong, he's right there in town."

"It's none of his business!"

"Personally, I don't think it's any of *my* business either, but here you are, telling me all about it so..."

"'Cause I can't tell Caleb."

"I see."

"What? What do you see?"

How, in the midst of talking about Belinda Baxter's favorite sex club, did they wind up on the subject of Caleb? Is this how it's going to be now that her so-called brother is back in town? All Caleb, all the time, no matter how she tries to avoid focusing on him and his broad shoulders and the shift of his powerful legs in those ass-hugging jeans and those—

"Baby girl, I don't care if you go to this club. Hell, I don't care if you sleep with five guys in one night—*I need the room please, Nora. Just another minute, okay?*"

"Awesome," Amber whispers.

"All I care about is that you don't go looking in the wrong place for what you really want."

"That's kinda what the place is about, apparently."

There's a long pause before her mother says, "I don't understand."

"Belinda says they teach you about who you really are and what you really want. So who knows? Maybe I'll come away realizing this true love thing isn't for me after all."

"Yeah, you'll come away with a newfound love of handsome male hookers, in which case Belinda better give you a raise."

"Ouch, Momma."

"It may not sound like it, Amber, but I hope whatever this place is, you have a good time. And I hope that's *all* you have. Because that's really all you need right now. A very good time."

"Thanks, Momma."

"And Amber?"

"Yes, Momma."

"If you do have a good time, I don't want to hear another word about it."

"Deal!" Amber says brightly.

5

"Are you gay, dude?"

Caleb stares across the bar at his old friend, waiting for the guy to crack a smile.

Danny Patterson stares right back as if all he did was ask the time.

Apparently it was a serious question. Thank God nobody else inside Watson's heard it.

"No, I'm not gay," Caleb finally answers.

"You just never seemed that into Theresa is all."

"Well, we weren't in love. That's why we got divorced."

"I got that. So why marry her in the first place?"

"I don't know. Convenience?"

"Since when is marriage convenient? Especially if you don't love the person?"

We're not always supposed to be with the one we really love, Caleb thinks, but he doesn't say it because he knows Danny will just respond with more pushy questions.

Also, Danny hasn't shut up yet.

"Unless, you know, the dad's threatening your life 'cause you got the girl pregnant, in which case you do it 'cause staying alive is convenient. But...wait a minute! You didn't get Theresa pregnant, did you, 'cause I don't re—"

"Danny, you're twenty-three and you've been engaged three months. Quit lecturing me on marriage."

"Three or four sentences isn't really a lecture, if you ask me."

Which I didn't, Caleb thinks. *But you drove an hour out of your way to have a drink with me so I'm gonna be polite and not clean your clock today.*

People who watched too much daytime television liked to say Danny Patterson was *on the spectrum*. But as far as Caleb was concerned, implying someone had Asperger's syndrome was just a fancy way of shaming them for not talking to you like you were their boss.

He'd first met Danny back when they were both working on the Proby Ranch outside Surrender, Montana. The kid was fresh out of high school then, so Caleb had blamed his 5-Hour Energy drink demeanor on the blissful ignorance of youth. But Danny's older now and a cop, and still he chatters away like a five-year-old who doesn't know when to stop bugging his parents during a long car ride.

"So," Danny said.

"So what, Danny?"

"Are you gay?"

"For the second time here, which I'm hoping will be the last. I'm not gay. Why are you asking me this?"

"'Cause women catch on fire the minute you walk into a room and you're still single."

"I'm a huge player."

"You're not. You hooked up with one girl in the time I knew you before you married Theresa."

"I'm not a fan of women on fire."

"You're evading, sir. A guy who looks like you…well, it's just not normal for you to fly solo for this long, Caleb."

"Unless I'm going full *Brokeback Mountain* in secret, you mean?"

"Pretty much. Yeah."

"Well, if this is your way of telling me you think I'm good looking, then thank you, Danny. And I'm sorry I'm not more excited about that information, but, see, the thing is, *I'm not gay*."

"Eliza's got a gay brother and the dude's awesome. Good looking guy too."

"Son of a… Is this some kind of fix up?"

"What's wrong with that? What are you a homophobe or something?"

"What's wrong with it is that a good friend of mine is accusing me of lying about who I am. I'm not gay, Danny, and I'm not married to my ex-wife anymore 'cause we both moved on. It was a mutual decision, alright?"

"And you both moved on 'cause you were never in love with her to begin with and apparently she wasn't in love with you either. I guess that's supposed to make sense?"

"Danny, I'm fixin' to add some Drano to that Heineken if you don't shut up!"

"Just hate to see you alone is all," he says. He shakes his head with a faraway expression that says he's thinking about his new fiancée. Again. Because these days, he doesn't think about much else.

"I get it. You meet the love of your life and suddenly you're everybody's matchmaker. You're whipped, *dude*. That's all."

"Frat boys called it whipped. Grown-ups call it engaged."

"Sounds like something Eliza told you."

"It is," he says with a smile, as if his fiancée's corrections feel as good as her shoulder rubs.

"Serves you right for hooking up with one of your old teachers."

"Alright, now. Don't up the creep factor. You're sounding like one of the old gossips back home."

Danny's hearty slug suggests the gossips back in Surrender are bothering him more than he cares to admit. Caleb isn't surprised. In towns big and small, a ten-year age difference between lovers will make most people talk. But when the woman's the senior partner, people tend to freak out even more.

"Is it just talk or are y'all getting some real grief over it?" Caleb asks.

"Oh, just the usual busybodies, claiming we got together when I was a teenager and she was my teacher."

"Did you?"

"Hell, no. Back then, she pretty much wanted to chuck me out the window."

"Why's that?"

"'Cause I asked too many questions, apparently."

"You don't say."

"Only reason I give a damn is 'cause Eliza seems to give a damn, and after everything she's been through, I don't want her to have to give a damn about much besides being happy."

Caleb knows only part of the story, the part where Eliza's bastard ex got her involved with some nasty guys who didn't make it out of Surrender alive. There are about eighteen different versions of the story floating around Surrender. Every time he calls someone and tries to get the real scoop, he gets a totally different account. Whatever happened, Eliza and Danny survived without injury, and now they're in each other's lives for good. That's all that matters. More importantly, he'd rather get off the topic of their personal lives altogether before he has to answer any more questions about his own.

"Have you tried bringing her an apple every day? Maybe that'll cheer her up."

"Oh, that's real original, cowboy. How 'bout you sing me some of that old Van Halen song while you're at it?"

"Just trying to make light of the situation. Small towns can be tough."

"Yeah, well, Surrender's alright when the MacKenzies have your back!"

The way Danny says it, he makes Surrender's most beloved family sound like the mafia. They're anything but. Thomas, the doctor of the family, is the only MacKenzie Caleb had ever spent much time with, probably because he'd been willing to drive out to Proby at a moment's notice to treat even the first signs of an infection or a sprain among the ranch hands. If Thomas MacKenzie's generous spirit ran in the family, no wonder most of Surrender thinks he and his brothers hung the moon.

"Is that really why you came back to Dallas?" Danny says. "'Cause small towns can be tough?"

"Got family here," Caleb says. "Now I've got a family business, looks like."

"You never called this place your family business before."

"Danny, does Surrender have some intelligence agency that hires you to track down all the former ranch hands in the area and find out about their lives? 'Cause this is getting kinda intense, friend."

"Nah, I told you, Conference of Local Law Enforcement Agencies is at the Hyatt downtown this weekend and I'm representing my hometown." Danny taps one closed fist against his heart as if there's a shiny policeman's badge there.

"And you always like to kick off a conference by giving an old friend the third degree?"

Danny sips his beer and stares at Caleb.

"I was going to fix you up with Eliza's brother," he finally says.

"Danny!"

"Well, if it means anything, I lost the bet."

"The bet with who?"

"Eliza. I told her all about you and she's sure you're straight."

"She knows me better than you do, apparently."

"She also says your heart's on lockdown 'cause you already met the woman you want to give it to and you're convinced she won't take it."

Way better apparently.

"So who's the girl who got away?" Danny asks. "Is she married?"

If Annabelle hadn't picked just that moment to set an armful of invoices and order forms down on the bar with a loud *thunk*, Caleb might have faked a seizure.

"Here's everything you asked for," she says

"Whoa, you might want to get a filing system there," Danny says

Annabelle gives Danny a long stare, then turns it on Caleb.

"Who's the child with the mouth?" she asks Caleb.

"Old friend," he answers. "Just ignore him."

He reaches out with both arms so he can draw the mountain of lose paperwork closer to him without spreading it across the bar.

"Name's Danny Patterson, ma'am, and it just so happens I'm an officer of the law."

"In Dallas?" she asks.

"Nope. A beautiful little town in Montana called Surrender."

"Then shut up. You're out of your jurisdiction."

Danny gives Caleb a broad smile and says, "I always forget Texas is the not nice part of the South."

"And I'm the not nice part of Texas," Annabelle says. "So, Guy I Was Actually Talking To, this here's about six months worth of invoices and orders from my amazing former employer. As you'll be able to see, he forced us to use a cut-rate produce company even though every other batch they brought us was spoiled and also, he spent about seven thousand dollars on consultants to research"—she dug into the pile and read from the invoice in question—"the latest in jukebox technology. And by consultants, I mean members of his horrible band who Googled stuff about jukeboxes. Probably while hung over."

"I suppose I can't get you to file all of this stuff," Caleb asks.

"You can. For about forty dollars an hour."

"Oof," Danny says with a groan. "Pricey!"

"You know, normally, it takes people more than fifteen seconds to get on my nerves," she says.

"Oh, I don't believe that for a minute, Annabelle," Caleb says with a smile.

They just stare at each other while Danny looks back and forth between them like a kid expecting his parents to break out in a screaming match.

"I don't file, cowboy," Annabelle finally says. "I've got about a dozen chicken fried steaks that need to be battered before we open for dinner. But I'd be happy to take you back to the dish cabinet where he stuffed all the invoices for the past two years."

"Lord," Caleb groans.

"Nobody said being a knight in shining armor was easy," she says. Then, to Danny she adds, "Have a good one, Deputy Diaper. Enjoy those puppy dog eyes while you got 'em. I can already see the crow's feet starting."

"I love a woman who can make me feel small," Danny says after she's gone.

"You realize I'm calling you Deputy Diaper forever now?"

"Knew it the minute she said it."

"Want to do some filing?" Caleb asks.

"No, thanks. Knight in shining armor? She made it sound like you came home to rescue a lady, not a bar."

Don't look up. Don't let him see your eyes. He'll put two and two together and figure it out.

"Danny, unless you want to help me do some filing, you need to get gone."

"I love filing!"

"Danny, I was kidding. It was great to see you, buddy, but I need some time to pull things together here."

He's hurt Danny's feelings, and it makes him feel like crap. Truth is he's got all the time in the world to file these stupid invoices. Well, all the time in the world until tax day. But Danny's like a dog on a scent. Worse, he's following the trail right to a place Caleb needs to stay buried, and there's only one damn way Caleb can think of to stop him.

"Alright, well," his buddy says, sliding off his barstool. "Try to make some time to come down to the Hyatt this weekend so we can hang."

"Sure thing, buddy."

"And, you know, sorry if I asked too many questions or if I talk too much."

"Nah, man. It's work. That's all. Just gotta get back to work here."

"Sure. Sure. I get it. Good luck, you know…with all of it, I guess."

All of it. Including the stuff you won't talk to me about.

Caleb nods.

Danny nods.

Then he's out the door but not before giving Caleb a glimpse of his wounded smile.

He just stands there for a while, feeling like a royal shit.

He should have known this would be the hardest part. The questions. People noticing.

He didn't stay a loner for this long because he couldn't control himself; he'd never do something stupid where Amber was concerned.

His self-discipline's always been good. Abel Watson, his only real father, is to thank for that. But his feelings and his anger about his feelings, those are another matter entirely. Making sure they stay hidden now that he's back in Dallas, that's going to be a lot harder than getting Watson's books in order.

Sometimes, when he'd had a few too many with the guys he'd worked with up in North Dakota, he'd mention the woman he couldn't have, the one it would never work with, even though he wanted it to. Desperately. And if anyone pressed for more details, he'd just tell them the woman in question, the one he never named, had gone off and married someone else, which had been true then.

It wasn't true now. And if he'd known that, he might never have come home.

This isn't just fear squeezing his chest. It's a kind of terror, the same terror he always feels when someone brushes the sand off that deep, buried place inside of himself.

In his memory, he's back on the side of a winding country road on that awful night when everything changed. Abel's shaking him by both shoulders and asking him what he'd do to have a family. A *real* family. And then there's darkness. Darkness and branches and a whole lot of other stuff he doesn't want to think about.

He doesn't drink after people. It's a rule. But panic attacks call for an exception to pretty much every rule, so he downs half of Danny's abandoned beer in several swallows.

It helps a little, but only a little.

Maybe I should have let Danny believe I was gay, he thinks.

If he'd had any gay friends, he'd have put the question to them. What's harder, being gay or in love with the woman the State of Texas considers to be your sister?

When his phone rings, it gives him the crazy sense that he's been caught.

It's the woman the State of Texas considers his mother.

"Miss Tina?"

"We're not having this conversation," she says immediately.

"Okay. You want me to hang up?"

"No, no. I just… What I'm about to tell you, you need to act like you heard it from someone else."

"When?" he asks.

"What?"

"*When* do I need to act like I heard it from someone else? Right now or later?"

"When you do something about it, that's when."

"I'm real confused right now, Miss Tina"

"Okay, well, let me unconfuse you. Amber's about to do something crazy and I need you to stop her."

6

"Heroin?" Belinda asks.

"*What?* No!" Amber answers.

"Okay. What about cocaine?"

"Oh my God. Never."

Brow furrowed, Belinda stares at Amber like she's a cop and Amber's a suspect who will crack at any second. But they're not in an interrogation room. They're in the dining room of Amber's house and Belinda's holding a wine glass, not a notepad.

Next to them the wall is studded with bright spots where they just took down every picture featuring Joel. Or even a tiny piece of Joel. Amber tried to contest the removal of a big sky sunset over Chapel Springs on the grounds she wasn't 100% sure the elbow in the bottom right corner actually belonged to her ex, but Belinda insisted.

"Are you sure you went to college?" Belinda asks.

"Yes, I'm sure."

"Not even one little bump at an office party?" Belinda asks.

"I didn't even know they were called bumps. And the only office parties I've been to are yours."

"That's not an answer, honey."

"Belinda, I do not sniff cocaine!"

"Alright, there's my answer. No one calls it *sniffing* cocaine."

"I thought you came over to talk about The Desire Exchange."

"I did, and to erase all evidence that Joel Claire ever set foot in this house."

"And I appreciate that, but why are you asking me about my drug history?"

"I just need to know if you have any allergies."

"To *cocaine?*"

"They're just gonna give you a little something to relax you while you're there."

"Belinda, I do not do drugs!"

"Oh, come on. You never smoked a joint?"

"Not one I liked. No."

"Well, as long as you keep an open mind, I guess."

"Why would I need to keep an open mind if they're gonna drug me?"

"You'll have to have an open mind to *take* the drug, sweetie."

"I have a headache," Amber groans.

"Want a Percocet?"

"No. I've had too much to drink today, thank you."

Amber can't remember the last time she's heard tires squealing on her quiet residential street. But that's exactly what she hears now. Tires squealing.

"So has someone else apparently," Belinda mutters.

Headlights swing across the front windows of her house, headlights belonging to a large pickup truck which pulls into her driveway so fast, the front bumper knocks over one of her trash cans.

"Is that him?" Belinda asks. "Is that Joel? If it is, get my purse."

"Why?"

"'Cause my gun's in it."

The shadow that strides past the front windows is over six feet tall. But it's missing its familiar cowboy hat.

"It's not Joel," Amber says quietly.

"Who is it?" Belinda calls after her as she heads for the front door.

She opens it. Caleb lowers his hand. It's curled into a tight fist and he had the side of it aimed at the door, not his knuckles. A polite knock wasn't his plan. His sandy blond hair is mussed. His broad chest is heaving with big, fearful breaths. If she hadn't just witnessed his hijinks with the truck, she would have assumed he ran clear across Dallas to get to her house.

Gone is the confident guy who struck down Joel that afternoon. He's forgotten whatever words he was practicing on the ride over, that much is clear. He looks fearful and boyish, and together, they make him look innocent. Over six-foot-four, chorded with muscle and somehow innocent. Dangerously innocent.

"Oh, my," Belinda says. "You weren't cheating too, were you?"

"Belinda, this is my brother. Caleb, this is my boss, Belinda Baxter."

There's a second or two of shocked silence before Belinda says, "You have a *brother?*"

"On paper," Amber says.

Caleb flinches. It sounded terrible, the way she said it. But she couldn't think of another way to make the obvious chemistry between them seem less dirty and wrong.

"I was afraid I wouldn't catch you before you left," Caleb says.

"Oh my God. Momma told you?"

"You told your *mother?*" Belinda cries.

"Please don't go," Caleb says.

The quiet authority of his request shoots through her bones. This isn't the sauntering Caleb who can deliver a precise punch powerful enough to knock a man off his feet. This is the Caleb of fifteen years ago—needy, hungry.

"Why not?" she asks before she can stop herself.

He stares into her eyes. His lips part but nothing comes out.

For a few seconds, the only two things in Amber's world are the two of them and the years of unspoken feelings between them.

"Miss Baxter, I don't mean to be rude, but do you think I can have a moment alone with Amber?"

"Of course," Belinda says, grabbing her Gucci purse off the foyer table. "I'll just, you know, take a walk into the middle of the nearest freeway now that Amber's mother thinks I'm a freak."

Caleb steps aside to let Belinda pass, gives the woman a polite nod. Once she's behind him, she gives Amber a look full of wide-eyed confusion. Then Caleb gently shuts the door with one hand. Now it's just the two of them, alone together for the first time in years.

"It's a terrible idea," he says.

"Why did she tell you?"

"Because she wants me to stop you."

"That's not true. I talked to her this afternoon and she told me she wanted me to go."

"Well, she must have changed her mind," he says.

"Well, I haven't changed mine."

"A sex club?" he bellows. "What are you? Crazy?"

"Since when are you so full of judgment? I've never seen you in church!"

"And I've never seen you in a sex club!"

"Have you been to that many? Who knows? I could have a whole secret life you don't even know about."

"I know who you are, Amber. I know *how* you are."

"And what does that mean?"

"Amber, you stayed a virgin until you were nineteen. That puts you in the, like, one percentile of girls in our high school."

"How do you know that? I never told you that!"

"I had my sources."

"You were keeping tabs on my virginity? That's rich. I thought you were too busy starting fistfights outside Valley View Mall so you didn't have to feel anything."

"And you were too busy tending to my wounds 'cause it gave you an excuse to look at my chest."

"Get out of my house!"

"Amber—"

"Get out!"

He bows his head. A lesser man would ignore her request, but he knows he's bound by it.

"I shouldn't have said that," Caleb whispers. "I'm sorry."

He turns to leave.

"You know, I forgave you a lot because you lost a lot. But don't you pretend for one second that you joined our family with a smile and a thank you and that was that. Those first few years, it was like living with a tornado. You were *impossible*! And you were nothing like the guy I'd..."

He turns away from the front door. "The guy you'd what?"

"All I'm saying is that even if I'd wanted to..."

"Wanted to what?"

He's closing the distance between them. Her head wants to run from him. Her soul wants to run to him. Her body's forced to split the difference. She's got no choice but to stand there while he advances on her, nostrils flaring, blue eyes blazing.

"Tell me why you really don't want me to go," she hears herself whisper. "Tell me why you—"

He takes her in his arms and rocks them into the wall, so suddenly she expects her head to knock against the wood, but one of his powerful hands cushions the back of her skull just in time.

His lips meet the nape of her neck, grazing, testing. It's hesitant, the kiss he gives her there, as if he's afraid she's an apparition that will vanish if he tries to take a real taste.

He gathers the hem of her shirt into his fist, knuckles grazing the skin of her stomach. She's trying to speak but the only things coming out of her are stuttering gasps. She's been rendered wordless by the feel of the forbidden, by the weight of the forbidden, by the power of the forbidden.

It's the first time they've touched since that night on the boat dock, if you don't include the light dabs of hydrogen peroxide she'd apply to the wounds he got fighting, usually while they sat together in the kitchen, her parents watching over them nervously. So many years living under the same roof and they never shared so much as a hug after that night, nothing that might risk the feel of his skin against her own.

And now this.

Now the intoxicating blend of the cologne he wore as a teenager mingling with the musky aroma of his belt and boots. Now the knowledge that he'd asked after her virginity years before, that the thought of her lying with another man had filled him with protective, jealous rage then just as it does now.

She feels boneless and moist. One of those feelings isn't an illusion.

If this is what it feels like to be bad, she thinks, *no wonder so many people get addicted.*

"Tell me," she whispers. "Tell me why you really don't want me to go."

"I am," he growls.

He presses their foreheads together, takes the sides of her face in both of his large, powerful hands. It's torture, this position. It's deliberate, she's sure. It keeps her from lifting her mouth to his. Keeps her from looking straight into his eyes. He's fighting it, still. Just as she's fought it for years.

She parts her lips, inviting him to kiss her.

"Please," he groans. "Just, please *don't* go."

"Caleb…" She reaches for his face.

She's reaching into open air.

The door slams.

He's gone.

By the time she realizes what's happened, the truck's engine has already started. His headlights swing across the front of the house.

"You son of a bitch," she whispers to no one. "Coward, bastard son of a *bitch!*"

But real anger, the kind of anger she feels toward Joel, can't make it to the surface through all the other emotions she's feeling.

She wasn't nuts. She wasn't some deluded freak who'd made too much out of one kiss twelve years before. He'd wanted her as badly as she'd wanted him, and he'd been just as tortured by it. They'd had all of the anger and fighting of siblings, but with none of the loyalty and companionship. To try for either of those things would have awakened desires her father had declared off limits. Still, every argument they'd had, every time they'd forced themselves to look away from each other, every frustrated attempt they'd made to connect since the night his parents died, had just been another step in one long dance of desire leading up to this very moment.

But what *was* this moment?

Where the hell are they now?

Would he disappear again? Maybe for ten years this time. Or twenty!

Her father—*their* father—was gone, so why is this still so hard?

Dazed, she walks in circles around the living room while these questions assail her. She's holding her phone in one hand, waiting for anything. A text. A call. An e-mail. Something from Caleb that proves she didn't just imagine what happened.

Part of her wants to cry, but every time she starts, the smell of him, the feel of him, the sounds of desire and struggle that came from him turn her sadness into something more like exhilaration. Even the speed with which he left is proof that everything just changed. And maybe it will keep changing. And maybe changing means no more running and no more avoiding and no more shame.

Maybe.

But he still fucking left.

No text. No missed call.

What did he expect her to do? Chase him down the front walk, screaming his name?

The front door creaks. The truck hasn't come back so it can only be one person.

"Girl," Belinda says quietly.

Amber had completely forgotten her boss was lingering outside.

"When do we leave?" Amber asks.

"Uhm. Never."

"What?"

"You're not going, honey."

"Why? Because I told my mother?"

"Nope."

"Because Caleb doesn't want me to?"

"Nope."

"Then *why*, Belinda?"

"Because you don't need to find out what you want. You already know. He just stormed out of this house."

"He's my brother."

"On paper, you said. So what's that mean? Adopted?"

"Pretty much."

"Well, is he adopted or isn't he?"

"Yes. My parents adopted him when we were fifteen."

"I see... Well, people will talk, but they always talk, so who cares? And if you ever want to get married, you just dissolve the adoption before you—"

"Belinda, it's not that simple!"

"It is if you want it to be, Amber."

"Belinda. Come on, now. You promised me and I want to go. Seriously!"

"No, you don't, Amber. You want to avoid what you're feeling for this man *again*. And forgive me for saying it, but it's starting to look like the last time you avoided it, you wound up jumping into marriage with a cheating, lying bastard."

"Oh, come on! That is way too simplistic. You don't—"

"Honey, if you've got something that good knocking on your door here at home and you won't let him in, nothing they're going to show you at The Exchange is going to help you either."

"You don't even know him."

"I know how you two look at each other. And trust me, if there was someone in my life who looked at me like that, I'd never turn my back on him. Unless, you know, we were about to try a little—"

"He's the one who left."

"You told him to!"

When Amber shoots her an angry look, Belinda throws her hands in the air and says, "Oh, come on. You know I'm an eavesdropper. Stop acting all surprised every time I do it."

"I told him to tell me why. Why he didn't want me to go."

"And he did. Don't worry. I only watched part of it."

She sinks to the sofa, fully intending to sit, but she goes over backward the second her butt meets the cushions. Suddenly she's sprawled out just like she was when she arrived home earlier that day, her breaths feeling more like ideas than actual grabs for air.

"Shit!" Belinda says. "We missed one!"

Belinda takes a framed photo of Joel, in full fishing regalia, off the wall just above the mini-bar. She looks for a place to put it, doesn't find one that meets her needs and shoves it in her purse.

"I'll toss it out the window on the ride home," she says.

"Am I fired?" Belinda asks.

"No. Why do you always go to that place? Do you *want* to be fired?"

"No. I just want things to…change."

"Oh, honey. That's not your problem. They're changing all around you. What you want is for them to change on your own schedule, and trust me, that's never gonna happen. I got all the money in the damn world and even I can't slow time down. I mean, I can fill it with spa treatments, but that's not the same thing."

"What are we talking about?" she asks.

"Nothing. We're stalling. Like you've been stalling for, well, a good decade, it looks like."

"Fine. I'm not going to The Desire Exchange."

"Because you don't need to."

"I'll have to take your word for it, considering I still don't know what the place even is."

"And you never will. Because you, Amber Watson, already know good and well what you want. You're just afraid of it. And you're going to have to get over that fear all on your own. However, I'm happy to give you some time off to do it."

"No," Amber says. "I need to focus on something."

"Yes. And that something is you." Belinda starts for the front hallway. "I don't want to see you for five days. Take a drive down to Chapel Springs and see your momma. Maybe ask her why she thought it was a good idea to squeal on you to your *alleged* brother."

"What does that mean?" she asks, sitting up.

"Five days, Amber. Show up at my house before then, I'll take a shot at you. I swear to God."

"Wait. What did you mean about my mother?"

By the time she makes it to the front hallway, Belinda's already out the door.

"Does anyone else want to storm out of my house tonight?" Amber calls out. "Maybe one of the neighbors?"

A barking dog answers from next door.

She dials her mother's number.

Voicemail.

Fifteen minutes later, she dials it again.

Voicemail again.

She can't remember the last time her mother let her go to voicemail.

Her mom hates going to the movies, maybe because the nearest theater is forty-five minutes away. She also covers so many positions at The Haven Creek Inn, she never turns off her ringer.

Amber would love to be worried about her mother; she really would.

But she's not.

Because her mom's hiding, that's all. And that's why Amber heads for her bedroom and starts stuffing her favorite weekend bag full of blue jeans, halter tops, and T-shirts. First thing in the morning, she's got a date with a few hundred miles of blacktop and a little town called Chapel Springs. And if her mother calls back before then, well...Amber's got voicemail too!

7

If only he hadn't touched her.

If he hadn't touched her, he could leave her in his rearview right now, along with Watson's, Dallas, and the entire State of Texas. Maybe he'll hit Colorado this time. Or Canada. Canada isn't that much farther, but maybe an international border was just what he needed to protect his heart.

But there's no way he can go that far now.

Because he'd touched her.

And it wasn't like he'd had to either.

There were other ways he could have kept her from going to some crazy sex club.

Like reasoning with her. Or teasing her. Or begging her.

Telling her how he really felt, that should have been the last option. The absolutely dead-last, nuclear apocalypse option. And touching her? Well, that was beyond the nuclear option. That was a "zombies are breaking down the front door and the only way out is through the nearest window" kind of option.

And yet he'd gone ahead and done it anyway, touched her like he was some idiot teenager who couldn't control his hormones. He'd also tasted her, inhaled her scent, felt her heat on his skin. Sensed that her hunger for him was equal to his own. Heard that hunger with his own two ears, a vibrating pulse under her every desperate breath as he'd held her in his arms.

And now it's all falling apart. Now he's flying down a Dallas freeway with all the windows in his truck rolled down because he's hoping the wind will drown out his crazy thoughts. He's been driving for hours now, aimless circles around the city. Sometimes he'll head in the direction of old landmarks, old places he used to visit, but as soon as he gets close, he forgets about them altogether and goes back to thinking of Amber. Amber's eyes. Amber's skin. Amber's anger. Amber's passion.

Bye, bye scrapbook, he thinks angrily.

Over the years, he'd come up with all sorts of ways to keep his feelings for her under control. But the thing he called the scrapbook had been the most effective.

Early on, after he'd moved in with the Watsons, he'd forced himself to think of her only in her most unflattering moments. Her furious expressions during dinner table fights after which Abel would send them both to their rooms; her shuffling walks to the coffee maker first thing in the morning, replete with hay bale hair and baggy pajamas. The times a cold or the flu turned her into a red-faced phlegm machine. Out of these awkward, everyday moments, he'd made a scrapbook which he opened whenever Amber, the wickedly smart doe-eyed girl he'd fallen in love with that long ago summer, threatened to tilt him off his axis.

The scrapbook had not been without its problems, however.

Every now and then he'd try sliding in an image of how awful she'd looked the night her appendix burst. But the cruelty of this, using one of her most painful moments to dampen the fires of his desire, shamed him into further confusion. Worse, it would often backfire, serving only to remind him of how he'd wanted to protect her in that moment. How he'd wanted to take her into his arms and carry her down the stairs once it was clear it wasn't just a stomachache, that she was truly and terribly sick. Instead, he'd shouted for Abel and Tina. When they'd burst into her room, he'd hung back, shaking and trying to hide tears, but refusing to break the rule they'd both set for each other, however silently.

No touching. No grazes. No brushes. No hugs. No kisses, even on the cheek.

The scrapbook is as good as burned now. Now, every time he thinks of her from here on out, he'll see the pale creamy skin of her throat bared, her lips parting for him, inviting him to taste. Fuck that. He'll see that smoldering intensity in her stare when she said *Tell me why you really don't want me to go.*

Sometimes he'd hoped that if they ever did make a move on each other, they'd realize instantly their desire was an illusion. Kind of like prison love, or some outdated teenage fantasy they'd held on to for too long even though it had lost its fire years before. They'd try to kiss each other again and crack up laughing because the whole thing would seem ridiculous.

Some days he hoped for this. Other days he feared it.

When he finally did make his move, everything was very real. All of it. Too damn real.

Danny Patterson answers his phone after the first ring. All Caleb has to say is that he needs to meet, and Danny's giving him directions to the hotel, right down to which escalator he should take to get to the lobby bar. Maybe it's the tone of Caleb's voice that does it.

Caleb pulls into the motor court at the Hyatt Regency, hands the keys to his truck to the first valet.

Dealey Plaza and the Sixth Floor Museum are just a couple blocks away. Caleb knows this because Abel took him there several times when he was a kid.

Inside the hotel, there's a soaring atrium with a sloped glass ceiling that allows you to look right up at the glittering orb that is Reunion Tower. Caleb knows this because Abel brought him here to see visiting friends when he was a kid.

And that's half the problem, isn't it? In Dallas, Abel is everywhere, because Abel loved Dallas as much as he'd loved his own children. *Both* of his children.

Danny's waiting at the top of the escalator, a beer in hand. He'd probably have one for Caleb too, but he knows Caleb barely drinks. Caleb prepares himself for some smartass comment about how wrecked he looks. Instead, Danny steers them to a table and chairs. Rowdy law enforcement types fill the bar. Men, mostly, patting each other on the back, sharing loud war stories about shootouts and crazy arrests. Glass elevators whisk people to their rooms on the floors above.

The place is loud as hell, but Caleb hears the racquet as if he's underwater. Underwater and struggling to breathe.

"I did something terrible," he finally says.

"You finally put the moves on the sister who isn't really your sister?"

"Are you kidding me? You knew the whole time?"

"Figured it would mean more if you said it," Danny says with a serious nod.

"*What* would mean more?"

"I'm just kidding. I left my room key at Watson's and when I called back, Annabelle answered and I got the story out of her."

"Which story? Wait! *Annabelle?* She hated you!"

"Nobody hates me. They just need time to…get used to me, that's all." Danny frowns and takes a sip of beer. "Do you hate me?" he asks, suddenly sounding twelve years old.

"You think I would have called you if I hated you? I'm having a breakdown here."

"You're not having a break*down*. You're having a break...*in*. Wait. That didn't come out right. What I'm trying to say is—"

"Just stop trying to say stuff and listen, Danny."

"Oh. I get to listen now. Does that mean you're actually going to talk about what's really going on with you?"

"In a minute. What did Annabelle tell you?"

"That you two were made for each other. That you were practically in love by the night your parents died and when Abel adopted you, it screwed you both up."

"Screwed us both up? Is that what she really said? If Abel hadn't adopted me, I woulda been homeless. Or living with my aunt in Oklahoma City while she turned tricks right in front of me in her trailer."

"So, homeless, basically," Danny says.

"Yeah," Caleb answers.

"But still."

"Still what?"

"I'm just repeating what Annabelle said!"

"Okay. Fine. What else did she say?"

"She said she'd call and give you updates on the bar 'cause they wanted you to come back. That they knew Amber's husband was a piece of dog shit, and she only married him so she wouldn't have to deal with how she felt about you."

"*Annabelle* said all this?"

"Yes, Caleb. Apparently you're the only one who had a hard time figuring any of this out."

"I didn't say I hadn't figured it out. I just don't know how to fix any of it."

"Same thing. Anyway. She also said there's only one thing keeping you apart."

"Yeah. She's my sister."

"No, Abel. She says both of you are in a boxing match with his ghost. Her words. Not mine. Says you both think if you got together you'd be crapping on his memory."

These words hit him like a sucker punch, and that's a good thing. A sucker punch is exactly what he needs to wake up.

"Wish I could say out of the mouths of babes, but these are her words, right?"

"Yeah, also, I'm, like, four years younger than you, dude."

Danny smiles.

"You're a good guy, you know that, Patterson?" he hears himself say. The words come out of him before he can measure them, but it's the night for following his instincts, apparently, and saying them out loud makes him feel good. "I give you a lot of grief, but you're a good guy."

"Aw, shut it."

"Seriously. I was a dick to you today at the bar, and here you are taking time out from your friends to listen to me whine."

"Listening to you whine ages me," Danny says with a broad grin. "That's a good thing, right?"

"Well, now you know why I've been such a loner."

Danny spits up beer. It takes Caleb a second to realize the guy's laughing at him.

Once he finishes coughing, Danny says, "Dude, you were never a loner. You were always having the other hands at Proby over for cookouts at your cabin. You'd organize all the trips into town. Second an injury looked like it was infected, you were on the phone to Thomas MacKenzie. The reason I went to see you today is 'cause pretty much everyone you met back in Montana wants to know how you're doing.

"You're not a loner, Caleb. A wanderer, maybe. But not a loner. Just 'cause you've been running from one woman your whole life doesn't mean you're not a people person. You're one of the biggest people people...or persons... Oh, hell, I don't know how to say it. But you know what I mean. You love people, is what I'm trying to say. That's why you're not going to be able to run from her for very much longer."

"Maybe it's not her I'm running from," he says.

"What's that mean?" Danny asks.

Even though it's not his intention, Caleb finds himself looking from happy couple to happy couple. Some of them are leaning in to each other, so close it looks like their eyeballs are about to touch. Whenever he's in a crowded place, his attention seems to go right to the nearest happy couple, and no matter how hard he fights the urge, his gaze lingers on them while the Goddess of Envy places her cold, invisible hands around his throat.

There were moments with Theresa. Moments when it seemed like maybe the two of them could pretend their way into being in love. Moments when, if you didn't know any better and you saw them together in a bar, you might have thought they were as happy and contended as most of the couples in the Hyatt's atrium bar looked to Caleb right now.

But for the most part, they were just lonely. Like him, Theresa had convinced herself that true love, the kind you saw in movies and read about in romance novels, was something the universe only offered to other people. People who had their shit together. People who didn't have so many wounds.

And that's what had held them together for a while. A shared belief that the right one, the one for them, had been placed permanently off limits, so why not make a go of the one who was in front of you? That, and their matching wounds.

Back then, if you'd asked Caleb why he couldn't be the one Amber loved, he would have told you it was her decision, her choice. After all, she's the one who'd gone and married someone else. What more proof did you need? Now he knew that was a lie, a lie he'd told himself so he could get comfortable with his decision to run.

Now he'd seen her desire for him, seen it right where it had been lying just beneath the surface for going on twelve years.

She wasn't the one standing in his way.

Abel was.

And therein lay the unavoidable contradiction that had defined Caleb's life—the man who had saved his life was also the one who had shamed him out of pursuing his heart's desire.

"Caleb," Danny says softly. "You still here, man?"

"The night my parents died, we'd just kissed. For the first time."

"You and Amber?"

"We'd been building toward it all summer. She was… When I'd look at her that summer, something would happen to me. It was like everything about her was more vivid. More *there*. And when she'd look at me, something would happen to me too. I could feel it in my chest."

"You were falling in love with her," Danny says

"I was fifteen."

"Yeah, you were fifteen and falling in love with her."

"But…"

"But, what?"

"I took her down to the boat dock with me so I could show her the moon. 'Cause I'd told her how beautiful it looked over the lake at night and she said she wanted me to show her. And 'cause…"

Motherfuck, he thinks as his vision blurs. *Goddamn motherfuck shit. Crying right here in the middle of the bar.*

"I knew my father was gonna die. And so did she. And she knew I couldn't sleep and she didn't want me to be alone when I was lying there awake in the other room, so I took her down to the boat dock and when I kissed her it was like… When I kissed her, it was like there'd never been a thing called pain. Like I didn't even know what the word meant. It was like… It was like she was the only thing that existed."

"She still exists, Caleb. And she's getting divorced."

"I'm not finished," he says, hating the gruff sound of his voice. But if he stops to apologize, he knows he'll lose his nerve. Knows he won't finish the story. And if he can't do anything else right tonight, at least he can do that, finish the damn story for the first time.

"Few minutes later, Abel got the call about my parents and he came and got us. I don't remember much after we got back to the house. Except her holding me. I remember that. I remember lying on the bed crying my eyes out. I remember her reaching up and taking my hand. I squeezed it, I think. I squeezed it 'cause even then I wanted her to know that she still existed for me. That she would always exist for me. And then…"

One time he was horseback riding in the mountains near Proby outside Surrender. His mind had wandered as he took in the gorgeous view. At the last possible second, he'd seen the horse's hooves perched at the edge of a hundred-foot drop. For a few minutes, he hadn't been able to do anything except quiver and stare into those aspen-fringed jaws of death. That's how he feels now.

"Next thing I remember, I was in the car. Abel was driving. But Amber wasn't there. He said he was driving me to the airport. That a friend of his had a plane and was going to fly us back to Dallas. And all I could say was, Where's Amber? I remember saying it over and over again. At first, he didn't say anything. Then he just pulled the car over, got out, and pulled me out of the passenger seat. We were in the middle of this dark stretch of woods where there wasn't anything for miles and he was just shaking me, shaking me and saying all kinds of angry things. He was so mad I couldn't tell at first that they were questions he was asking me.

"Did I want a real family or did I want to end up drunken white trash, dead on the side of the road like my father? Did I want to listen to my dick the way my father had listened to the bottle? 'Cause that's what it would mean to be with Amber. Amber was going to be my sister and if I fucked that up, I wouldn't have nothing, he said. No family, no home. *Nothing.*"

Danny curses under his breath. Is he trying to contain his reaction because he doesn't want Caleb to stop telling his story? Caleb's not sure, so he keeps talking.

"And I just kept yelling at him over and over again, no matter what he said. Where's Amber? Where's Amber? And he drew back like he was going to hit me."

"Did he?"

"No. He drove off and left me there instead."

"For how long?"

"I don't know. I didn't have a watch on me. I thought I could find my way back to the lake house, but I was wrong and I ended up in the woods. Sun was rising by the time he found me. He was half out of his mind by then. Sobbing and crazy and begging for my forgiveness. And what choice did I have? Only other option was my aunt, and she probably would have left me on the side of the road and never come back. Or sold me to some freak for meth."

"Jesus, Caleb."

"He wasn't a bad man, Danny. He lost one of his best friends that night."

"Still."

"He worked so hard to try to keep his men together after they came back from Iraq. But my dad, he was the one Abel couldn't fix. It's not like he took his hand to me. My real dad did that plenty."

"He left you in the woods, man."

"He came back."

"After he scared the living shit out of you."

"I wasn't scared. I was something else."

"What?"

"Lost."

"And then you were what...found?"

"Something like that, yeah."

"Bullshit. He created the situation just so he could fix it. You wouldn't have been lost if he hadn't thrown you out of the car."

"He wasn't thinking like that. He was upset."

"You're talking like him because you're thinking like him, and if you're thinking like him it means there's a part of you that still believes what he said to you that night. You think if you go after Amber, you're going to end up a drunk like your father, dead on the side of the road. You really believe that, Caleb? You really think everything you want is dangerous just 'cause your dad was an alcoholic?"

He can't answer.

"How many things in life have you wanted and not gone for because of what Abel said to you that night?"

"Sometimes you decide that something else is more important."

"Like what? Moving? Again?"

"It's not that simple."

"Are you a drunk, Caleb? Do you wake up without knowing where you are? Do you lose track of your truck? Do you get in fights you can't remember starting? Wake up counting the minutes until your next beer?"

"No," Caleb whispers.

"Then you're not your father."

"Still…"

"Still, *what?* You're not your father, Caleb. And Amber isn't booze. Abel was wrong. He was wrong that night. Hell, lot of people would say what he did to you was downright abusive, but I'll leave that for you to decide. Point is, he didn't understand what a drunk really was, and he sure as hell didn't understand you."

"He was a good man who made a mistake," Caleb says. "And God knows, he made up for it later."

"Yeah, okay. I never met him so I can't say. But if twelve years later, you're not going after the love of your life because you're still buying into the bullshit he said to you that night, then the one making the mistake is you, buddy."

Caleb wishes he had something in front of him. If not a beer bottle, at least a glass or a bowl of chips. Something he could grip. Something that would make it easier to resist the urge to punch Danny in the face.

Danny stares right back at him. Baby-faced, for sure, but also cool as a cucumber under the pressure of Caleb's furious, unrelenting glare. The kid's not backing down. And so Caleb breathes through it. The anger, the desire to argue with his words and his fists. The desire to turn over the table.

Because Danny's right.

Abel's not standing in his way.

Amber's not standing in his way.

He's standing in his own way.

"It's almost one in the morning. My room's got two beds. You want to crash here tonight?"

"I'd like to drown you in that fountain is what I'd like to do."

"Good. That means you know I'm telling the truth."

8

Amber wakes from a dream of kissing Caleb to find her mouth full of bedsheets.

Her bedroom is dark save for the alarm clock, which tells her it's only three thirty in the morning.

This was the best she could do? Two hours of fevered dreaming that left her feeling jittery and wired, as if she hadn't slept at all and didn't really need to?

A text or call from either Caleb or her mother would have lit up her cell phone's display. Even though it's a dark patch on her nightstand, she grabs for it anyway, unlocks it just to be sure.

Nothing.

Well, if I *can't sleep!*

She dials her mother's home number.

How many voicemails has she left for the woman already?

Shouldn't she start the clock over now that she's had somewhat of a night's sleep, however terrible? Fifteen unreturned voicemails the night before, which would make this current call the first official call of—

"For the love of the baby Jesus, Amber, it's three thirty! Go to bed! You can yell at me in the morning!"

"It *is* morning!"

"Sunup, then!"

"How dare you rat me out to—"

Click.

Enraged, Amber throws the phone across the room.

For a terrifying instant, she's afraid it's going to smash into the opposite wall and break into several pieces. Instead, it lands on the foot of her bed with a weak *thump*, a reminder of why she never played softball.

All hopes of sleep dashed and the source of her current troubles unwilling to remain on the phone with her for longer than ten seconds, Amber sees only one option.

A brief, frenzied shower and two Diet Cokes later, she grabs the weekend bag she packed the night before and heads to her Sentra. She's got the driver's side door half open when she shuts it suddenly, heads back inside the house, grabs four Diet Cokes out of the fridge, gets back in her Sentra and speeds off in the direction of the freeway.

If she manages to drive straight through to Chapel Springs, she might catch her mother before her first cup of coffee. She speeds up, hoping to get there sooner. Too bad she didn't bring a pair of cymbals with her. Maybe she can stop and pick one up along the way.

An hour south of Dallas, her eyelids start to get heavy.

Are you kidding me? Now? Now I'm tired?

It's still dark out, which is why she doesn't notice the approaching thunderstorm until lightning forks on the horizon. Lightning. Her least favorite thing next to menstrual cramps and snakes.

Also, I'm tired. Really tired. And getting more tired. And even though this fact seems dramatically unfair, saying so over and over again to herself isn't making her any less tired.

A few minutes later, sheeting rain washes the windshield. The taillights in front of her become vague, bleeding suggestions. She's got another two and a half hours to Chapel Springs. Maybe three, if this weather keeps up.

If I were home in bed, I'd be wide awake and staring at the ceiling. But now I'm getting sleepy. So very, very sleepy.

Traffic slows to a crawl. Traffic! At four in the morning.

Unfair. All of it. So unfair. She just wants to get to her mother, that's all. All she wants to do is rant and yell and scream at her mother for breaking her confidence, thereby blowing the lid off a potful of feelings she's tried to keep at a low simmer for twelve years.

She's going to get herself killed if she doesn't pull over.

The motel she pulls into is the kind of place where people go to have one-night stands with men who love face masks and recreational chainsaws.

"Can I get a room until this storm lets up?" she asks when she goes into the front office.

The kid behind the front desk looks like a twelve-year-old playing a game of Let's Be A Motel Clerk. He's even slicked his hair into a perfect side part.

"We're not that kind of place," he says.

"Not what kind of place? Aren't you a motel?"

"Yes, but are you in some kind of trouble? Is somebody following you?"

"What are you? Twelve years old? I just want a room. I don't do lighting all that well, okay?" And then she catches sight of herself in the reflective glass behind the clerk and realizes she looks like she's been struck by it.

No wonder the kid seems terrified. Apparently she started thinking about something else when she was in the middle of drying her hair after her frenzied shower, because even after getting rained on, it still looks wild and teased, like she's a backup singer out of an 80's music video who's been run over by a car. Only now does she remember that she actually started to put makeup on before thinking *I don't need to be wearing makeup to strangle my mother.* Problem is, she didn't bother to take off any of the makeup she applied before changing her mind, and now half of her face is running with it, making her look a little like that dog that used to sell beer when she was a girl.

She's startled back to the present by a metallic thud.

The clerk drops a key on the desk in front of her.

"You may not believe this, ma'am, but I'm a Christian and as such I kinda feel like it's my duty to keep you off the road right now. You can have the room for free 'til sunup."

"Thank you. I guess."

"Also, I'm twenty-nine."

"Yeah, sorry."

Only when she's almost to the room does she realize the clerk didn't say anything about keeping her safe during a storm. He probably meant it was his duty to keep the road safe from her.

The room's actually not as bad as she feared.

And there's a phone.

A phone with a number her mother won't recognize on caller ID.

"I've got bail money," her mother answers, sounding bored. "Just tell me where you're holding her."

"How could you?" Amber cries.

"How could I what? Where are you?"

"I'm driving to Chapel Springs to murder you."

"You're going to murder me right now?" her mother asks.

"No, I was going to murder you once I got there."

"Are you still drunk?"

"Stop deflecting!"

"So you are still drunk."

"I am *not* still drunk. It's been hours since I've had a drink."

"Human hours or dog hours?"

"Now who's being sarcastic?"

"I am! Because it's five in the morning."

"I called you fifteen times and you didn't return one of my calls. Don't act like I'm being crazy for no reason."

"Okay. Fine. But we can agree that you're being crazy?"

"Sure. Fine. Alright."

There's a silence on the other end. Thunder rolls outside. She can just make out the rustling of her mother's comforter. She's sitting up in bed, a sure sign she's getting ready to talk some truth.

"So what did he do?" her mother finally asks.

"What did *who* do?"

"Caleb. What did he do when I told him?"

Amber's so caught off guard by her mother's directness and the resignation in her voice, she can't manage a response at first.

"Oh my God," she finally says. "Belinda was right. You told him for a reason. You were trying to make him jealous."

"Pretty much, yeah. Did it work?"

"I'm not going, if that's what you mean."

"To the sex club place thing?"

"It has a name, but who cares? No. I'm not going. So yeah, you got your way."

"Did *you?*"

"What does that mean, Momma?" But she knows exactly what she means, and the knowledge makes her voice sound shaky and weak.

"Honey," her mother says. "I'm just gonna cut right to the point because it's five in the morning and I don't actually know where you are and I'm just hoping it's someplace you're not about to get murdered or washed into a ditch. But twelve years ago your father made a decision about what would be best for Caleb and what would be best for you. He made it without consulting me or anyone else, but he made it with his heart and the absolute best of intentions, I can assure you. And you know what, Amber?"

"What?" she asks.

"He was wrong. He was dead as a doornail wrong. And if you accept how wrong he was, you will not besmirch his memory or his name."

I'm just tired, that's all, she thinks, tears blotting out her vision as she sinks to the foot of the bed. *I'm just tired and about to get divorced and stressed. That's why I'm crying. That's why I can't speak.*

"I'm going to tell you a story. I never told you before because as soon as Caleb grew up it stopped being my story to tell. And it was one of your daddy's greatest regrets. But the night Tim and Abby were killed, when you all were up at the lake house and he decided to leave you there and take Caleb back to Dallas, he lost control. He and Caleb were in the car on the way to the airport and Caleb wanted you to come and he wouldn't stop asking for you."

Amber's too startled by this information to even gasp. She'd always assumed Caleb's grief for his parents had effectively killed his desire for her. Had taken whatever he'd felt for her on the boat dock that night and sent it into exile. But he'd asked for her. Even in the midst of all that pain, he'd asked for her.

"Well, he threw a fit is what happened," her mother continues. "And your father pulled the car over and he shook him. He shook him and he said all sorts of terrible things. He told Caleb that our family was his last shot at ever having one. He told the boy that if he ever acted on his feelings for you, he'd lose that shot forever, that he'd be out on the street.

"And then he left him there. He drove off like he wasn't coming back. Of course, he had a change of heart instantly. He was out of his mind with grief over Tim and Abby, you see. But by the time he turned back Caleb was gone. The boy had tried walking back to the house, but he got lost and it took your father hours to find him.

"Darling, your father had to do things in the Marines he never wanted to talk about. Hard things. But I can assure you, he didn't regret any of them the way he regretted what he did to Caleb that night. He spent the rest of his life trying to make up for it. But he was convinced the only way you two could care for each other was if you were siblings, not lovers, and nothing I said ever changed his mind about that. He said brothers and sisters last forever, but teenagers fall out of love all the time. And Caleb couldn't afford to have you fall out of love with him or vice versa. 'Cause what Caleb needed more than anything was a family and you had to be part of that family, no matter what. And like it or not—and I didn't like it, not one bit— there was only one way your daddy knew how to make that happen. Unfortunately, it was the wrong way.

"I guess I always thought you two would just grow out of it. That one day, you'd both be grown-up enough that you'd see y'all were made for each other and that your father had just been delaying the inevitable.

But it's not that easy, apparently. Even with Abel gone, it's still not that easy. I guess I understand. Sometimes, if we wear them long enough, chains can seem like clothes."

Her mother goes silent for a minute.

"You still there, darling?" she asks.

"Yes," Amber croaks through her tears.

"Aw, honey. It's easier to get over the mistakes of a bad man 'cause you can just dismiss the man. But the mistakes of a good man? Those are much harder to contend with."

Someone pounds against the door. Amber jumps and leaps to her feet.

"Darling?" her mother asks. "You alright?"

Amber peels back one corner of the curtain. The man outside is so tall he blocks out the overhead light. And he wears a dripping Stetson and a light jacket.

"He's here," Amber says in disbelief.

"Who's there?" her mother asks. "And where is *there?*"

"Caleb's here. I'm in a motel and Caleb's here."

"Well, that escalated quickly."

"It's not like that."

Another series of pounding knocks, followed by Caleb's voice bellowing her name.

"Okay, well, I guess if I'd wanted more of an explanation I could have returned one of your ten thousand calls."

"I should…"

"Yes, you should. You let that man inside, darling. You just go right ahead and let that man inside."

Amber stands there for a second listening to the dial tone, realizing that as soon as she puts the phone back in its cradle she'll be crossing a point of no return.

When she opens the door, he reaches up and pulls his hat off so she can see it's him. The gesture sends raindrops spraying from the hat's brim to the pavement beside him. How long was he out in the rain looking for her? How is it possible that he's here at all? There's fear in his big, beautiful blue eyes and his tense mouth suggests he's having trouble breathing.

"What the hell are you doing?" he asks.

"What are *you* doing?"

"Following you."

"Well, come inside."

When he steps across the threshold, he seems to fill the room. He sets his cowboy hat down next to the tiny boxy television. Then he begins to slide out of his jacket, one arm after the other, slowly, so as not to send raindrops spraying everywhere. And now there's just the sound of the rain pounding the roof and the occasional roll of thunder and the occasional flash of lightning as the man she's resisted for years greets her in an anonymous motel room.

He looks bigger than he's ever looked before. Maybe it's the room. Maybe it's how close they're standing. Maybe it's what they did to each other just a few hours before. Or maybe it's because she's seeing him as a teenager, a teenager clawing his way through dark woods, sobbing and grief stricken and desperate to find his way back to the only family he'll ever have.

"How long have you been following me?" she asks.

"I was parked outside your house. I was going to wait until you woke up but then you sped off so I followed you."

"Why didn't you call me? You knew I was awake once I was driving."

"I thought you were going there, that place. The sex club."

"I see."

"Are you?"

"She won't take me anymore."

"Your boss?"

"Yeah?"

"Why's that?"

Because of you, she thinks. *Because she knows I'm in love with you.*

"My mother..." The words leave her. She hasn't closed the door all the way. She moves to it, shuts it with a final-sounding click.

"Is she okay?" Caleb asks.

"She told me what Daddy did to you the night your parents died. She told me about the woods. And what he said to you..."

Caleb looks away as if he's been slapped. He's never done that before. Looked away from her with a turn of his head so pronounced it seems as if some loud noise in the bathroom has stolen his attention.

"He did something to me that night too," she says.

He looks back to her as quickly as he looked away.

"He took me aside and said I couldn't go with y'all back to Dallas. He said he knew what happened down on the dock and that things were going to have to change. Did you know? Did you know he said something to me too?"

"No," he whispers. "No, I just thought..."

"Just thought what?"

"I just thought…me being in your house, I thought it was too much for you, is all. And I thought you didn't want to be with someone whose parents had just died. I thought my sadness…I thought my sadness drove you away."

"Tell me that's not what you thought," she says, blinking back tears. "Please tell me that's not what you thought for *twelve* years."

"It's not your fault. We didn't tell each other anything. Nothing real, anyway. So how could you have known?"

"'Cause you were afraid if we did anything other than fight all the time, that he'd throw you out on the street. Was that it?"

"Something like that. Yeah."

"How long were you in those woods, Caleb?"

"I don't know." His voice is hoarse. He makes no attempt to hide his tears. "But when I watched you marry Joel, a part of me felt like I'd never left 'em."

He's got her in his arms before she's closed the entire distance between them. He's so much bigger, so much stronger and more confident than the fifteen-year-old she kissed years before. And his embrace alone is intoxicating. The feel of his powerful hands stroking her back warms her entire body. His breaths rustle her hair, sending gooseflesh down her spine.

"Is it really going to be here?" she asks.

"Is what going to be here?"

"Our first real kiss is gonna be in this crappy motel room?"

"Second," he says.

"Still."

"Well…" he says, and then he releases her suddenly, and for a second she's terrified she's infuriated him by being too casual and sarcastic about a moment that could change them forever.

Caleb hurls the door open, but he only takes several strides before he turns to face her, arms thrown out, the heavy rain pelting his shirt and jeans, soaking his hair instantly.

"There's no full moon," he cries over a roll of thunder. "But I've waited this long, I could kiss you anywhere."

She runs to him, leaving the door open behind her.

There's no resistance. No fumbling. Their mouths meet instantly, then their tongues follow suit, and suddenly she's cradled in his powerful embrace, so powerful he's lifting her up onto the balls of her sneakers.

Several minutes go by before she even realizes she's soaked from head to toe, and even then she doesn't care. All her life she's been afraid of lightning. But not now, not here. It could strike several feet from where they're standing and still she wouldn't be able to pull herself away from this kiss, this kiss she's imagined countless times. And if lightning struck the two of them, then at least she'd die doing what she'd most wanted to do since she was a teenager.

Her hands come to rest against his chest. She realizes she's been pawing at the collar of his shirt, that the top few buttons have come undone, and there's his hard muscle, glistening with rain. And it's like a second glorious revelation. She doesn't just get to act on her love for him now, she gets to act on her lust too.

"See," Caleb says, voice gravely, "we don't always need a full moon."

"That thing you said…"

"What thing?"

"About kissing me anywhere. Was it a promise?"

"Let's go inside and see."

9

"Take it," she whispers as Caleb pushes her closer to the bed.

He gives her another desperate kiss, then grips her chin in one powerful hand.

"Take what?" he rasps.

"All of it," she says.

He kisses her again, drags the hem of her shirt up over her chest with both hands, then his fingers trace the edge of her breasts. His thumbs find her nipples and apply two pinpoints of pressure through the fabric of her bra. He rubs smaller circles, then bigger circles, then smaller. Then bigger. Smaller. Bigger.

"Take all of *what*, Amber?" He says this with the tone of a schoolteacher who knows the answer and is trying to get his pupil to say it.

"All of me," she says.

He gives her a slight shove. She bounces on the mattress. When his weight comes bearing down on her, she realizes what she's trying to do. She's never spoken to anyone like this in the bedroom before. She wants to unleash him with her words, to set him loose upon her body.

She doesn't want to work for it. She doesn't want to ride; she wants to be ridden. More importantly, she doesn't want to think. Doesn't want to hesitate or falter or do anything but let him taste every inch of her. She wants him to take her the way he's always wanted her, the way she's always *hoped* he wanted her, and when he does it, she wants him to blast all thoughts of other people's expectations from her mind.

If he were resisting, this approach would seem selfish on her part, childish even. But her commands have unleashed a torrent of growls and hungry kisses from the only man she's every truly craved.

His fingers claw at the button of her jeans.

The door swings open behind him. Rain swirls in the room.

No one fills the doorway. Caleb just failed to close the thing all the way during their lustful dance back into the room.

He leaps to his feet and shuts the door so hard with both hands, the building shakes.

"Fuck this door!" he shouts.

"Or fuck me instead," she says before she can think twice.

"Dirty girl," he growls, crawling onto her, hands braced on the mattress on either side of her, bending down to give her deep, lingering kisses. "Dirty, dirty girl," he growls.

"Not unless you make me…" She hesitates over her next words, wondering for a second if it's too much, if it might blow the whole thing. But when he unbuttons her pants and a flush of deliciously chilly air bathes the crotch of her panties, lust devours fear. In a hissing whisper, she says, "Not unless you make your little sister a dirty girl."

His eyes widen. He grips her chin in one hand, stares into her eyes, as if this label were a kind of challenge. Did she just blow it? The passion uniting them is more than just some suppressed incest fantasy, and maybe her wording was too careless and heated and rushed. Why bring up the labels her father forced on them both? To destroy them, that's why. To cast them into the fires of their newly released passion so they can be incinerated and replaced by something altogether different, altogether new. And maybe that's what she really means when she tells him to make her a dirty girl—change me. *Change us.*

He's kissing her like she's something altogether different, that's for sure. Then he licks his way up the side of her neck with the flat of his tongue while he palms the crotch of her panties gently with the heel of one hand, drawing figure eights that brush her clit at the top. She's clawing at the buttons of his shirt, pushing it back over his shoulders, chills racing through her at the feel of his bare, muscular skin beneath her fingers, beneath her palms, beneath her desperate, hungry grip.

There's so much of him. So much size, so much brawn. So much muscle and so much hunger. It feels like he's everywhere on her at once, the sheer size of him distracting her from the fact that he's just unfastened her bra and drawn it off her breasts with his teeth. Then he's suckling her neck until he finds a special spot that makes her legs rear up off the bed and wrap around his waist—a spot no other man has found. Then he's got one of her breasts in a powerful grip, squeezing it just enough that he gets the right angle on her nipple, which he tongues madly, then suckles, tongues madly, then suckles. And just when she feels consumed by this pleasure, just as he switches from one breast to the next, he peels the crotch of her panties back from her mound and fingers her folds, dazzling her clit for a few brief seconds before diving deeper into her wetness.

Awestruck, quivering, she watches as he pulls his mouth from her slick nipple, brings his fingers slathered with her juices to his nose and takes a deep smell. "There's my Amber," he whispers. He slides her fingers between his lips and sucks on them briefly. Tasting her. Savoring her. "There's my sweet Amber," he growls. Then it seems as if he can't decide between the lure of her pink, pebbling nipple or a deeper taste of the juices he just sampled as if they were divine nectar.

Breathless with suspense, she watches him. He senses this and his eyes cut to her. He smiles devilishly. He's got her right breast in one powerful grip and his other hand is rubbing lazy, cloying circles across her mound. "Let's see," he grumbles. "Decisions. So many tasty decisions." He flickers her nipple with his tongue.

But it's just a distraction.

In a flash, his still booted feet hit the floor. His hands grip her waist. He's got her jeans off in no time flat, and then her panties, and then, as if that weren't enough to make her skin catch fire, he grabs the back of her thighs, drawing her legs up and apart. And then he goes to work. And she screams. She literally screams.

No one's ever done it like this before. No one's ever devoured her with this outright abandon, this determination not to miss an inch. In his every move, in every flicker of his tongue, there is as much a desire to dominate as there is a desire to please. He even dips just below her folds, coming to the edge of a place no man has ever been. Each brush of this place causes her to let out a small cry, and each time she does, he locks eyes with her. The message is the same. No part of you is dirty. No part of us, of the way we've always felt for each other, is dirty. Not here. Not anymore.

His powerful hands slide under her butt, gripping her cheeks, lifting her off the bed so he can bend forward and get a better, more focused angle on her clit. She hears strange thuds before she realizes she's balled her hands into fists and she's striking the comforter on either side of her to keep from screaming.

Devoured. Consumed. Taken. Never before has she connected these words to the act of sex. Hell, she would have laughed at anyone who did. But they all describe exactly how she feels now. Caleb gives her clit a rest now and then so it doesn't go numb. He takes time to search her folds with his tongue and puckering lips, looking for new sensitive spots. The whole time he keeps his eyes locked with hers, searching for any evidence of new, unexpected pleasure in her expression.

It's not a certain spot that does her in. It's those eyes. Those eyes she spent so many years refusing to meet for fear of being drawn into dangerous temptation. Those eyes that stare into her own now. Those eyes that belong to Caleb, the man she was forced to call brother before she could claim him as her lover. Those eyes and his name, which escapes from her lips unbidden. Which she says again and again and again until the dam breaks and the hands she's balled into fists turn to claws and Caleb rears up, sucking harder.

He uses the arm he's braced under the small of her back to lift her further up off the bed. And as she cries out, he grunts sharply against her slick folds. She has some sense of what's happening, but part of her thinks it can't be true, and she can't exactly pause to investigate while in the grip of her own orgasm. But just the thought of it quickens the waves of pleasure coursing her limbs.

He's coming too, she thinks. *Is he really coming in his own Levi's?*

He pulls his mouth from her sex as if it were a struggle, stands erect suddenly. She's spent, boneless. For a few minutes the idea of moving seems an abstraction. Then she lifts her head and stares down at the foot of the bed. Caleb is just standing there, hair tousled and still rain slicked. The baffled expression on his face makes him look innocent, despite his God-like muscles. The bulge in his jeans is considerable. So is the wet spot.

"Son of a gun," he says. "Can't believe it."

"Seriously?" Amber asks.

She slides off the bed and hits her knees in front of him. He backs away, one hand going up to stop her as she reaches for the button on his jeans.

"No, no, no," he says, but he's laughing. "No. This is embarrassing."

"Don't be embarrassed. Show me your cock."

"This is the first time this has ever happened to me," he says. But he's moved his hands out of the way. "I swear."

She unbuttons his jeans. The idea that just the taste of her made him lose control like this is almost as gratifying as the orgasm that just pulsed through every cell of her body.

"Well, tonight's a first for a lot of things, isn't it?" she says.

Not once did she ever try to sneak a peek of him in the shower when they were growing up. The sight before her now is her thick, beautiful reward. The way his cock, still slick with his seed, peels away from his stomach once she pulls down his briefs makes it seem as if the thing is literally presenting itself to her. The only thing missing is a bow and a silver tray.

He laughs softly, still embarrassed. This display of vulnerability as he towers over her awakens as much desire in her as the ministrations of his skillful tongue. She closes one hand around the shaft. A small sigh escapes him. He's not laughing now. He's dead serious as he gazes down at her, fingers twining in her hair, biting his lower lip gently. He must feel exactly the way she did when he was deciding between suckling her breast or devouring her sex. She can feel the tension in his body, the desire to force her mouth onto him fighting with the desire to take in the sight of her, submissive and on her knees.

"You're a big boy, Caleb," Amber whispers.

"Oh, yeah. Well, you're a—"

Before whatever porn star line he was about to deliver can come out of his mouth, she takes his cock into her own. The sound that comes from his half groan, half cry, there's a tremble to it, the tremble of a strong, powerful man being shaken to his core. She's sure it's not just the physical sensations of his still sensitive cock sliding between her lips, but his surprise at having her suck his fresh seed from his shaft.

Both of his strong hands grip her head now. But he doesn't try to drive her; he's steadying himself, taking care not to pull her hair. There's a loud thud from above and she knows just what made the sound—his head slamming into the wall behind him.

Once she's cleaned him off, she pulls away. In response, he cups her face in both hands, even though his eyes are shut. He's drawing her gently to her feet. She's never done anything like this before. Never tasted the essence of another man in this way. Never wanted to before him. And the idea that she might have just destroyed his desire to kiss her pains her suddenly.

Too much, she thinks. *Too far. I went too fa—*

He kisses her tenderly, gently, at first. The way he holds her face as he does slays her thoughts and conquers her self-judgment and makes the motel room fall away.

"So long," he whispers. "I have waited so long for this, so long for you."

"I'm sorry if I—"

"No," he says, placing a finger to her lips. "No. There's no sorry here, not right now. That, what we just did, was nothing to be sorry for."

As to prove his point, he reaches down and before she realizes what's happening, he picks her up like a bride and carries her toward the bed. He lays her down gently, then settles down onto the mattress behind her, spooning against her, a reverse of the position into which they'd settled the night his parents died.

He rolls away from her. She hears his belt buckle clacking against the button of his jeans. When he spoons into her again, he's naked against her bare behind. The intimacy between them feels somehow sealed by this simple act. He's already spent. He doesn't seem to be demanding another go-around, and yet, he's disrobed just so she wouldn't feel more exposed than she currently does.

"The kid in the office said I had to be out by sunup."

"I paid him already," Caleb whispers.

"Seriously?"

"It's how I got him to tell me which room you were in."

"Good thing you're not an axe murderer."

"Good thing a night in the sack with me didn't rid you of your smart mouth."

"You got that right," she says.

"Good. I love your smart mouth."

"Do you?"

He reaches up, grips her chin gently and tilts her head back so he can look into her eyes.

"Do you know what I'm about to say?" he asks.

"That if we get anything from this bedspread you're gonna kill me?"

"No," he says with only a slight smile at her joke.

Whatever he's about to say, it's serious.

"You don't need to wait for me to say it, do you? I mean, you've waited long enough, haven't you?" he says.

"Caleb—"

"I love you, Amber Watson. I've always loved you. Even when I believed we could never be together, even when it hurt so bad to love you I couldn't see straight, I never stopped. I couldn't even try to make myself stop. It was true then, and it's true now. I'd rather spend the rest of my life feeling the pain of not having you, than spend one moment of it not loving you."

"You won't have to," she whispers. "You won't have to know what it's like to not have me ever again."

It feels as if someone else has spoken through her, but maybe that's what it feels like when you finally speak your truth. And when he kisses her, she feels like she's floating somewhere just above her body, but maybe that's what it feels like when you kiss the man you truly love.

"I love you, Caleb…"

And she stops.

She was about to echo his words. She was about to use his full name, just as he used her own, but now?

"Eckhart," he says. "My full name, my *birth* name, is Caleb Eckhart, and when I was fifteen years old, a good man named Abel Watson allowed me to live with him and his wonderful family and so when he adopted me, I changed my name to Watson. But that time has passed now. There's something new on the horizon. New and better. So as soon as we're back in Dallas, I'll get myself to a lawyer and find out how to change my name back to Caleb Eckhart, and you and I will be able to slow dance in the middle of Watson's and won't a soul be able to say a damn word about it. If that's what you want, of course."

She smiles.

"Do you want me to, Miss Watson?"

"Yes," she answers. "Yes. Because I love you, Caleb Eckhart."

People really can kiss like this, she thinks. *Long. Slow. Forever.*

"Caleb," she says a few minutes later.

"Yes, Amber."

"Don't get me wrong. This has been one of the best nights of my life. But I'm really slee—"

10

A phone rings close to her head.

Amber's not sure where she is at first. She rolls over and recognizes the motel room's corded phone, the same one she used to call her mother. But it's not ringing. That would be her cell phone, which is on the opposite nightstand.

She rolls in the other direction, grabs her cell, glimpsing the clock on the display as she brings it to her ear.

It's three thirty. Again. It's the afternoon version of three thirty this time, and she's not sure if this should make her feel guilty or not.

For nine hours she slept. That's probably a good thing. But she's alone. And that's not good at all.

She sits up, panic tensing her limbs.

"Hello?" she croaks.

"I take it you've changed your mind about my imminent murder," her mother says.

Just then, Amber sees the spread of items on the dresser next to the T.V. At first she assumes the cowboy hat is Caleb's, but it's way too small, and it's not the same color as the one he wore that morning. As the daughter of a man who ran a country music bar, she knows her Stetsons. This one's a royal Western, flesh-colored with a slender black band. Caleb's partial to a black skyline, where the band blends in to the dark fabric and the upturn along the brim is more severe.

The reason this hat is different, she realizes, with a skip in her chest, *is because it's mine. He bought it for me!*

"You're not answering so I assume that means you still plan to murder me?"

"I am not," she says, rushing to the bathroom mirror so she can see how she looks in her new duds.

Wow. Huge mistake. She still hasn't washed off her freak show makeup.

"Oh my God," she whispers. "Did we really have sex with me looking like this?"

"That was more than I needed to hear."

"Oh, cut it out. You were the instigator of this whole thing! Don't get all high and mighty now that you got your way!"

"I see," her mother says. "So crazy's getting replaced by sassy this afternoon. You are aware it's the afternoon, right?"

"I needed sleep."

"Where are you?"

"Some motel somewhere."

She returns to the dresser. Caleb's also left out a just purchased, folded pair of blue jeans—almost the right size, but not quite—and a T-shirt which, for a second or two, she's afraid has some dirty saying about riding cowboys written on it, but which turns out to be printed with the spare but lovely silhouette of a cowboy on horseback before a giant, setting sun.

Sweet.

There's also clean underwear and a fresh pair of socks and bottles of her favorite shampoo and body wash.

"Is Caleb with you?"

"I think so," she says. "I hope so."

She draws back the curtain, and there he is, sitting by the motel's woebegone swimming pool, a postcard of cowboy perfection with his hat tilting forward on his head while he—

"Caleb plays the *guitar*?" Amber asks.

"Lord, I hope not. All that strummin' and whining. Makes me want to drown myself in a creek."

"Momma. That's no way to talk about the guitar."

"Really, Amber? After your track record with musicians?"

"Is there a reason for this phone call other than to give me an apology you haven't given me yet?"

"Yes. Where are you?"

"I don't know. Some motel. We're about an hour outside of Dallas. I was on my way to you."

"To murder me. Yes, I remember."

"I'm still considering it."

"Yes, well, that's very interesting, baby girl. In the meantime, I'd like you to drive another two hours south because the pleasure of your company is being requested at The Haven Creek Inn."

"By who?"

"By your *mother*, thank you very much."

"And whose company is that exactly?"

"You and Caleb. Now I'm gonna get off the phone before you slip and tell me how big it is."

"*Momma!*"

"See you in a few hours, sweetheart."

She wants to join Caleb by the pool, but she also doesn't want to go out in public looking like a psychotic cowgirl who just survived the running of the bulls. She showers quickly with the products he just bought for her, each squirt of shampoo and body wash feeling like a kiss from the man who took the time to buy them for her.

Only once she's standing at the motel room door, clean and dressed, the cowboy hat he bought for her perched on her head, does the fear hit. Maybe he's sitting by himself outside because he's having second thoughts. The gifts could have been compensation prizes, not tokens of affection, and he could already be planning his next escape. He hasn't looked in her direction once. Is he rehearsing a little speech about how last night was a giant mistake?

Start walking, she tells herself.

By the time she's a few steps from the chain link gate, Caleb looks up from the guitar on his lap. As soon as his eyes meet hers, the fear vanishes. Everything about him seems relaxed and unguarded. Seeing her so close seems to brighten everything about him, from his smile to his eyes.

The storm's passed over completely, leaving behind towers of puffy clouds against a dome of blue. In broad daylight, the motel actually seems a little charming. The room numbers are all the same antique-style brass, the parking lot lines freshly painted. And the water in the pool looks clean, even if the pool itself is just a plain concrete rectangle fenced in by chain link.

"Thanks for the care package, sir," she says.

"You're welcome," he answers. "Hope you didn't think I was trying to brand you with all the cowboy paraphernalia. Nearest place I could find was a country western emporium, this being Texas and all. Although, I must say, you do look mighty cute in that hat."

"Thank you," she says. "So, guitar, huh?"

"Yeah, I've been taking lessons. Didn't want to come right out and say it, you know, given your history with a certain songbird."

"That's sweet. Thank you."

"You want to hear something?"

Uh oh.

"Sure, I guess."

"You guess? Well, that doesn't sound very enthusiastic."

"I am. I'm very enthusiastic. Play me a song, Caleb *Eckhart*."

With a big grin at the sound of his newly modified name, he gestures for her to take a seat on the lounger next to his. She does, wondering, *Is this going to be like one of those moments in a Nicholas Sparks movie?*

Caleb sucks in a deep breath. He grips the guitar's arm carefully, his chest rising and falling. He strums.

Something doesn't sound right.

He strums again and it sounds worse.

Oh, shit, Amber thinks, trying to freeze a plastic smile on her face.

"Aaaaamber," he says.

"Hello, Caleb!"

"Shhh. That's part of the song. It's about you."

"Oh. Okay. Sorry."

Caleb nods, takes another deep breath, and starts again.

This time, the strumming sounds even worse.

"Amber," he sings. "A-uhm-ber. She's like the mooooon."

Oh, shit, Amber thinks again.

He strums wildly, and if there's a connection between the notes he's singing and whatever he's doing to the guitar, only he can hear it. And she would like to stop hearing it. Very soon.

"She's like the moon, if the moon was hot and had breeeeeeeeasts."

"Put that thing down!"

Caleb cracks up laughing as he sets the guitar to one side. "I've never had one lesson in my life. Some guy left this out here and asked me to watch it while he went inside to take a call from his wife."

"Good, 'cause that was God-awful."

"But you really are like the moon if the moon had bre—"

"Shut up," she says.

He pats one thigh. "First have a seat right here, *sis!*"

A bolt of heat shoots up her spine. As she settles onto his lap, the hard muscles in his thighs flex. He curves an arm around her back. They're an hour's drive from anything she'd call home, but still, to be this intimate with him right out in the open makes her feel flushed and light-headed and a little giggly. In its own way, it's more intoxicating than much of what he did to her body earlier that morning.

"Now you really do need to stop calling me that," she whispers with a sly grin.

"You didn't seem to have a problem with the whole forbidden passion routine last night," he says.

"This morning, you mean."

"Details," he says.

"That's 'cause I was doing away with it."

"Us being brother and sister, you mean?"

"Yep."

"How's that?"

"Well, you know. By turning it into a little role-play game, it stops being a real label. I mean, people can role-play pretty much anything they want. Cops. Fireman. Cowboys. It usually means they're not actually any of those things."

"I am a cowboy," he says.

"That's true. But for the most part."

"I see. So role-play. Was that something they were going do out at Belinda's sex club?"

"If you call it that to anybody else, you'll probably get me fired."

"Sorry. Lips are sealed. Promise. I will, however, be willing to consider opening them for other more important activities." He gives her a gentle bite just above her collarbone, more like a light pinch of his teeth. She grips the back of his head, fights the urge to drive his mouth further down where it can nibble on her breast.

"The point is that's not what we are anymore, right?" she asks.

"That's right," he says. "That's very, very right. We did away with all kinds of things last night. Things that weren't working for either of us."

He rests his head against her chest. She's breathing deeply for the first time in days. Or weeks. Or months. Years, even.

"And today, at almost four o'clock in the afternoon, we're starting something altogether new," he says.

"Exactly," she answers. "New."

They hold each other for a while as the trucks blow past them on the highway.

"Can we start it by getting out of this motel?" Amber finally says. "I've kinda had enough of this place."

"Ah, really. I'm always gonna have a special feeling for it, you know, considering." He sits up suddenly. "What's it even called?"

"Something shameful, I'm sure."

Caleb spots the sign. "The Showtime Inn. Ha!"

"A shameful name for a shameful place," she says.

"Nothing shameful about what *we* did," he says, looking up at her. He reaches up and smoothes her bangs back from her forehead.

"I was only kidding," she says.

"I wasn't."

"Kidding about the motel, I mean."

"And not last night?"

"This morning, you mean."

"Details, details," he says with a grin.

She bends forward. He closes the remaining distance so they can kiss. "The details were important," she says. "I liked the details. Very much."

Footsteps slap the pavement nearby. A guy's heading toward the pool clad in swim trunks and a tank top, probably the owner of the guitar Caleb just used to fool her. He smiles at them both, a smile Caleb returns. Then Caleb grabs the back of her neck quickly and brings her ear to his lips. In a hoarse whisper, he says, "My favorite detail was when I found the spot right below your clit that made you whimper like a little kitten, and I sucked on it till you clawed the bed on either side of you like you thought I was going to tongue fuck you into outer space. What was *your* favorite detail, my little cowgirl?"

The guy's two feet away by the time Caleb finishes this filthy declaration. Her breath lodged in her throat, Amber straightens and gives the guy a broad smile. She sat up so quickly her cowboy hat almost came off, but she rights it just in time. Caleb's whispers have sent shivers of pleasure throughout her body.

"Thanks, partner," the stranger says as he picks up his guitar. "Hope you fooled her like you wanted to."

"I see," Amber says.

"Y'all make a cute couple," their visitor says with a smile, then he heads off back in the direction of his room, guitar in hand.

Because they've never heard these words before, said with such innocence and so free of drama, the two of them just sit for a while, soaking them in.

"So," Caleb finally says. "Where to?"

"Our presence has been requested at The Haven Creek Inn in Chapel Springs."

"Cool. I've never been."

"Really?" she asks.

"Nope."

"Well, it's certainly a day for firsts, isn't it?"

"Yeah," he says with a boyish grin. "When's seconds?"

"Bad boy," she says, then plants a kiss on his lips.

"So we heading out now?"

"I guess, yeah."

"You guess? What's troubling you?"

"I think we should head straight there. She sounded pretty eager. Maybe 'cause I threatened to murder her last night."

"Forgive me if I seem confused, but when someone threatens to murder me, I'm usually not in a rush to have them over to the house."

"You know what I mean. Last night we had words. I think she wants to make up for it."

"This morning, you mean."

"Exactly."

"Alright, well, still doesn't explain the long face."

"I just don't want to take separate cars, that's all," she says. "You and me, we've been taking separate cars our whole lives practically because I was so afraid to be alone with you. And now all I want is to be alone with you. So I don't know where we'll leave my car, but fact is, I want to ride with you and I'm not going if I can't."

Her pouty expression earns her a belly laugh from Caleb.

"Well, that's a lucky coincidence, miss, 'cause I don't feel like going if you don't ride with me either. And while we're speaking the truth, I don't feel much like letting go of you once we get there neither."

"Unless," she says.

"Unless what?" he asks, expression falling.

"Unless you try playing the guitar again, in which case I might run for the hills and never come back."

"Well, I'll just have to catch you then!"

She's not quite sure how he does it, but in an instant, he's standing and he's got her in both arms and she's got no choice but to wrap her legs around him to keep from falling. And just like that, he's carrying her across the parking lot and back to their room.

"Or you could just never let me go," she whispers into his ear as he walks. "That way, you don't have to risk me running in the first place."

"Sounds good to me, darlin'."

11

It's amazing what you can learn about someone after two hours alone together in the car, Amber realizes.

Like the fact Caleb's actually a smooth and focused driver, his antics in her driveway the night before not withstanding. Or that he likes country music way more than she realized, and when he sings along with it, he sounds a heck of a lot better than he did during his little comedy routine by the motel's pool.

She also feels blessed he's such a country fan because for the first time in her life, the love songs they're listening to seem written just for her. She doesn't find herself thinking things like, "Well, that's just lovely Miss Hill! But let's hear about a *real* marriage!" And when Chase Rice asks her to climb to the top of the water tower so they can kick it with the stars for an hour, it sounds like the invitation is sincere.

The troubles and pain of the last few days don't just feel miles away. Rather, with Caleb's free arm draped across her shoulders and a blazing big sky sunset off to the west, anything seems possible.

Do you have to have love to feel this way, she wonders, or is this how most people feel when they finally walk through the fires of a fear that's lain in their path for most of their lives? Love certainly helps, that's for sure.

Once it was clear her marriage was in a nosedive, she'd had fantasies of getting in the car and just driving and driving until she wound up in her own version of Chapel Springs, some suitable, peaceful refuge from a life defined by fear and hasty choices. But the trip she and Caleb were on now was of a different nature. They weren't driving away from something; they were driving toward her mother and The Haven Creek Inn, and the very real fact that people who cared about them both had wanted the two of them to get together long before they were willing to take the leap.

Some of those people, anyway.

Rather than stew over what her father might think of this new development, Amber slides out from under Caleb's arm so she can take his free hand in her own and hold it to her chest. He returns her grip, but his expression seems distant, more distant than someone watching the road.

"Listen," he says suddenly.

Uh oh.

"What?" she answers.

"This place Belinda was going to send you to," he says.

"Yeah?"

"Did you really want to go? I mean, I'm asking because you told me about what things were like with Joel, how he went cold on you in the bedroom, and then I kinda barged in and did my thing and... I just don't want to feel like I took something away from you. Something you needed before..."

"Are you asking if I needed to sow my wild oats?"

"Kinda. Yeah."

"So did it seem like there was something missing this morning? Did it seem like I was distracted while you—how did you put it? Tongue fucked me into outer space?"

He grins at the road and bites his lower lip and tightens his grip on her hand. He likes it when she talks dirty. She makes a note of that. Good thing the feeling's mutual.

"Is that a trick question?" he asks.

"Nope. Did I seem distracted?"

"You did not. You did not seem distracted."

"Well, there's your answer then."

"Still, I don't want to feel like I shamed you out of doing something you needed to do just 'cause the thought of you with other men made me want to break the door down."

"Well, if we're being honest here, the thought of you breaking the door down to keep me from being with another man kinda makes me want to do a repeat of this morning right here in your truck."

"Well, we can certainly add that to the list," he says.

"Good."

"You're asking me if you're enough, aren't you?" Amber says.

Caleb tilts his head from side to side as if he's considering her question, then he says, "Yeah. I kinda am, I guess."

"Well, I think that's sweet."

"Sweet?" he asks, grimacing.

"Yes. I think it's sweet that the most beautiful man I've ever met in my entire life, probably the only man I've ever really loved, just a few hours after giving me the best orgasm of my entire existence, is asking me if he's enough. It speaks well of your character. I don't want your head to get so big your Stetson won't fit."

"Sassy," he says, and gives her left thigh a hard, loud slap. "Sassy girl, Amber Watson."

"That's me!"

"But you're not answering my question."

"Well, the funny thing was, about five seconds before you pulled into my driveway last night I was about to throw in the towel on the whole idea."

"Why's that?"

"Well, for starters, Belinda wouldn't tell me anything about it. Honestly, I still don't know anything about it. I know it has a name, The Desire Exchange. I know that they were going to try to give me some kinda drug to relax while I was there, which I had *no* intention of taking. And I know we were supposed to be gone for two days. But that's it."

"But you said yes?"

"I said yes at first 'cause when Belinda talked about the place, she got this look in her eyes, like... I don't even know how to describe it. But I thought, here's one of the richest women I know, who could have pretty much anything she wants, and when she talks about this place, I don't know, it was almost religious."

"Huh," Caleb grunts.

"But she's the one who said I shouldn't go. And she said it after she saw the way we looked at each other. She said I didn't need the place or what they had to offer. She said what I needed was right there in front of me and his name was Caleb."

"Caleb Eckhart," he says quietly.

"Yep," she answers.

He smiles, brings her hand to his mouth and gives her fingers a gentle kiss.

They've passed through Austin. The rolling green landscape of the Texas Hill Country spreads out before them now, painted with oranges and deep reds by the westward leaning sun.

"There was one other thing," Amber says.

"What?"

"There was an application process and for part of it, I was going to have to write down my deepest sexual fantasy. Those were Belinda's words. *Deepest* sexual fantasy. The one I was afraid to tell anyone."

"You just have one?" Caleb asks.

"Dirty boy."

"Dirty girl," he answers.

They both stare at the beautiful countryside in silence for a few minutes.

"You can tell me, you know," he finally says. "Your fantasy, I mean. Doesn't matter how deep or how dark."

"Yeah? And then what?"

"I'll do my best to make it real. That's what."

He takes his eyes off the road just long enough to give her a devilish wink. Between this simple gesture and the promise he just made, her breath catches and her cheeks flame and her heart skips a beat. Maybe a few beats, she can't really be sure.

Why the hell not? she thinks. But as soon as she goes to speak, a cold weight settles down over her chest. A day before the fantasy would have seemed fairly tame, as sex fantasies go. Now, not so much. Caleb might not consider it so tame considering it involves being lost in the woods.

"Amber?"

"I'm working on it," she says.

"No rush," he says. "Maybe writing it down'll be easier, when you're ready."

"Maybe so."

Her heart's racing. If she doesn't tell him now, she'll feel like she's withholding something of value. But will the fantasy still work for her now, given the awful story she just learned of what her dad did to Caleb the night his parents died? The thought of Caleb forcing himself to act out some sort of sex scene that might stir such a painful memory, just because he's desperate to make it work with her, fills her with anxiety. For so long now, she's felt like little more than the victim of her husband's betrayals. She never felt like she was even capable of hurting Joel; that's how little the man seemed to care for her. But now, all of a sudden, she's responsible for someone else's heart.

"Hey," Caleb says, "did I push a little too hard there?"

"No," she answers.

"Prove it," he says, curving his arm around her shoulders, pulling her body into his as he drives confidently with one hand.

A few minutes later, the gates to The Haven Creek Inn come into view.

12

The Haven Creek Inn sits on a large hill that dominates the property's eighty acres of live oaks, sloping green lawns, and winding hiking trails. The main building, a two-story L-shaped structure of roughhewn stone, is perched on the hill's crown, the rocking-chair studded porches on its first and second floors commanding gorgeous views of the expansive landscape to the west.

Her mom asked them to meet her at the newest guest cottage, so Caleb drives past the inn's main building, past the half-circle of smaller guest cottages that dot the hill's gentle slope, past even the large, rectangular swimming pool framed by a smoother version of the roughhewn stone used in the main building.

In the early evening dark, Amber can see flickering candles lining the serpentine front walkway of the newest guest cottage. Each glowing candle bag is cut with the inn's logo, a half-moon partially shaded by tree branches. None of the cottages they pass on the way had string lights laced through the gutters of their shiny metal roofs as this one does. Her mother must have added this glittering touch just for her as well.

Just for *them*, she realizes.

And there's her mother, standing on the front porch, dressed in a white polo shirt bearing the inn's logo, the same shirt she always wears when she's on the job. She's flanked by two of her closet friends in the world.

Because she's only four foot nine, most people mistake Nora Donner for a small child from a distance. She's pushing sixty, but she has a child's energy level combined with a desperate desire to please. Some call her codependent, others simply call her kind. Amber's in the latter camp, and her mother goes back and forth between the two, which is probably why she and Nora have been close friends for years.

To her mom's left stands Amanda Crawford, the woman who had made The Haven Creek Inn a reality. She's Nora's polar opposite; a tall, slender gazelle to Nora's energetic pixie. The multimillionaire is also possessed of a classic beauty she maintains through an unassailable combination of good genes, good nutrition and, when necessary, the scalpel of a talented Austin surgeon with whom she sometimes spends romantic weekends she refuses to discuss.

Caleb kills the truck's engine. For a minute, the two of them just sit there, staring at the beautiful scene before them.

"Wow," Caleb finally says.

The hill country to the west spreads out before the cabin's decks like a vast, green sea. In the absence of city lights, a riot of stars is unveiling itself throughout the night sky. Now that they've parked, Amber can see more string lights wrapped around the trunks of the live oaks that watch over the cottage like sentries.

And that's when the tears start.

"Hey," Caleb says quietly, drawing her close with one arm. "Hey, you alright?"

"Yeah," she manages, wiping quickly at tears with the back of her hand. "It's just really beautiful, is all."

"I guess she really wanted us to visit," he says.

"Together. She really wanted us to visit together. That's the thing."

And then Caleb seems to get it. That every candle, and each string light, and the cottage itself, are all her mother's way of trying to make up for twelve years of misunderstanding and confusion and thwarted desire.

"Y'all going to get out of that truck?" her mother finally calls. "Amanda's gotta get home before her manicure melts."

"Tina," Amanda says, voice smooth as silk, "I do wish you would stop using my beauty against me."

"We better get out of the truck," Caleb says.

"Sounds like a plan."

Amber's halfway up the front walk when her mother says, "I don't see a gun so it looks like I'm going to be okay, ladies."

"Hug your daughter, Tina," Nora cries.

And so she does. And when Amber tightens her embrace, her mother tightens hers as well. They've been about the same height ever since Amber graduated high school. But her mother's got a lean, wiry frame from the laps she swims every morning. Her mane of salt and pepper hair is healthy and thick, but it's also threatening to come loose from its ponytail, so Amber adjusts her mom's scrunchee even as they hug. By the time they've parted, her mom's hair is back together again.

Tina stares into her daughter's eyes with newfound seriousness. "See," she says. "There are some things your mother's big mouth is good for."

"Thank you," Amber whispers.

"Don't mention it," she says, smoothing hair from Amber's face. "Just stay a while."

Caleb's introducing himself politely to Amanda and Nora, both of whom have moved so close to the guy it looks like they're about to manhandle him. When Amber steps up onto the porch, Amanda works to pull her stare from the towering hulk of a man in front of her. Then she places one hand on his shoulder gently as she steps past him. As soon as she makes eye contact with Amber, she wags her hand in the air as if the man were literally hot to the touch.

"Darling," Amanda says once she has Amber in her arms. "How you went twelve years without laying a hand on that hunk of burning love is simply beyond my ability to comprehend."

"Well, it was pretty weird, Amanda. I can tell you that."

"Uh huh. Whatever. Notice we gave you the cabin furthest from the inn. So have at him, sweetheart. Only ones eavesdropping are the birds. And the bees!" She gives Amber a light peck on the cheek. "Lord. I need to go book myself a massage. Y'all have fun now, ya hear."

Nora waits for Amber on the top step of the cottage's front porch, which makes her and Amber almost the same height. Almost. The tiny woman throws her arms out in front of her, shifting her weight back and forth between both feet. As always, Nora Donner's happiness is a force that cannot be contained.

"Oh, what do you say kiddo?" Nora cries as they hug. "*What* do you say?"

"Oh, you know, just getting divorced and hooking up with the man who used to be my brother. That's all."

Nora cackles.

"Well, we're so happy for you," Nora says, pulling away but holding Amber's hands in hers. "We are. We are. We really are. I mean, you know, Joel was just…" Nora pauses as if she's considering whether or not to add mint or rosemary to a glass of lemonade. "Well, he was just such a piece of shit, that's all. I wish there was a nicer way to say it. But there really isn't now, is there?"

"No. There isn't. He really was a piece of shit. In fact, I was just with him yesterday, and he still is."

"I'm so sorry, honey." Nora takes her hand and leads her to the far side of the porch. "Now listen…"

"Nora!" her mother calls out when she sees the two of them alone together. By then the tiny woman's already reached under her polo shirt and removed a glossy trade paperback she's been hiding inside the waistband of her jeans for Amber doesn't know how long. "Now if there's something about Joel that didn't seem quite right, something that seemed off in a way that was perhaps, nonhuman, I want you to read this book and tell me if any of it makes sense to you. You know, on a personal level."

The cover art features a tiny black silhouette of a man surrounded by swirls of star-filled cosmos that partially conceal a giant pair of black inverted teardrop eyes. The book's title is *The Stars Are Upon Us.*

"Now don't read it late at night because it might frighten you. But what it makes clear, darling, is that the infestation is already underway. They're already at the highest levels of government. There's evidence they're crossbreeding us. It's got pictures, see, in the insert in the middle. Pictures of the hybrid children. And honestly, I was thinking about Joel's facial structure and comparing it to some of these drawings and I think it's very possible he could be a hyb—"

"Nora, get that alien nonsense away from my daughter! She's on vacation!"

"Now your mother thinks this is nonsense," Nora explains gently. "But what I'm trying to say is don't blame yourself if you end up being taken advantage of by one of them. They're everywhere, you see. And they don't think and feel the way we do. It's not about Republican versus Democrat, sweetheart. This is about us versus the stars!" Nora points an index finger skyward and nods solemnly.

"That's really sweet of you, Nora, but I don't think Joel was an alien. I just think he was an asshole."

"Even so, read the book. It's very important."

"Nora Donner, men in white coats will be the least of your problems if you don't stop with that this instant!"

"Your mother likes to threaten me because she can't bear the truth," Nora says gently.

"I understand. Thanks for the book."

Nora gives her a peck on the cheek and more of that big smile, that smile Amber can never get enough of. Then, like a chastised dog, she walks into her best friend's outstretched arms, which curl vise-like around her upper back and begin guiding her away from the cottage.

Amanda has just pulled up next to Caleb's truck in one of those golf carts the staff uses to get around the property.

"Dinner service starts at six," Tina calls back over one shoulder.

"Please," Amanda purrs. "We're not going to see those two for hours. Days, even."

"Oh, you hush!" Tina hisses.

She and Caleb stand together on the porch like new homeowners, watching the golf cart speed off uphill.

"What was Nora going on about?"

She hands him the book. "She thinks you might be an alien."

"A good alien or a bad alien?"

"I'll have to thoroughly examine your body to be sure."

"Sounds like a plan," Caleb says with a grin.

He takes her by the waist and leads her into the cottage. On the console table inside the front door is a map of the property, across the top of which someone, presumably Nora, has drawn a giant smiley face next to the word, *Welcome!* Most of the cabin is decorated in creams and light browns, with sliding glass doors that lead to an expansive deck offering views of the sunset's last, dying rays. In the bathroom, the Jacuzzi tub is flush up against a plate glass window that looks out over treetops.

"Can we do my alien examination in this tub?" he asks.

"Sounds like a plan."

He takes her in his arms. Their lips are inches apart. "That's turning into a refrain with you this evening."

"What can I say? You're just bursting with good plans."

He kisses her, gently at first, then harder. Then he's holding her so tightly he's lifting her up onto the balls of her feet, and she realizes this is going to be one of those things he does that drives her wild. One of the many things he does that drives her wild.

"Easy, big boy," she says when they both come up for air. "We plan on taking a bath in that thing we better start filling it up now."

"Why? It'll only take a few minutes."

"Clearly, cowboy, you have little to no experience with Jacuzzi tubs."

"Oh, don't be silly."

Twenty minutes later, or as she'd prefer to think of it, three and a half make-out sessions later, they're sitting on the edge of a half-full tub, watching the water line rise gradually even though the faucet's gushing.

"Damn," he says. "You weren't kidding."

"Toldja."

"Alright, well, it gives me time to prepare something."

"What?"

"You'll see. I want you naked and in that tub by the time I come back."

"Is that an order?"

He grins, rises off the edge of the tub. He grips the back of her neck gently, then firmly. When she doesn't wince or ask him to stop, he tilts her head so she's staring up into those blue eyes she's spent so many years not looking into.

"Would you like it to be an order, little lady?" he asks in a deep, gruff voice.

Shivers dance down her thighs. The heat in her belly is poised to spread throughout her body. Images from the fantasy she still hasn't shared with him swirl across her vision before she blinks them back.

"That feels like a yes," he says.

He tightens his grip a little more. She gasps.

"I think I'm getting closer to that fantasy you don't want to tell me about. Am I right?"

He tightens his grip a little more.

"Am I, little lady?"

"Yes," she whispers.

He releases her suddenly, takes a few steps backward, and says, "Good. Then get those clothes off and get in the tub. I'll be with you in a minute."

On his way out of the bathroom, he dims the light.

Technically she's alone, but the act of undressing feels deliciously naughty given she knows who she's doing it for.

She leaves the faucet running as she sinks down into the warm water. A few minutes later, Caleb walks into the bathroom wearing a cowboy hat and nothing else. Their first lovemaking was so frenzied and rushed, she didn't have the time to study his body. Now she can clearly see every ridge of muscle, the light tattoo of old scars from his years of hard labor, and the heft of his cock and balls, which swing as he walks. Surrounded by the opulent bathroom's marble and polished stone, he looks like he walked right out of the dark woods and into her most secret chamber.

Only once he's settling into the tub across from her does she realize that his nudity was also meant as a distraction. In his right hand, he holds several sheets of hotel stationary and a slender coffee table book he lifted from the living room. And a pen.

In a neat pile, he sets all three items into the space between the window and the edge of the tub. Then, with a beaming smile, he slides them toward her with one arm. Before she has time to respond, he finds her wet, eager folds under the surface with one big toe and begins prodding at them gently but insistently.

"What could possibly be in that head of yours that you think I'd be too afraid to try?" he asks.

"Caleb…"

"Alright, well, if it'll make you feel safer, I'll add some ground rules. For me, I mean."

"Go ahead," she says.

"No other people. Although I'll be happy to play more than one role, if you like. Oh, and I won't draw any blood. Not 'cause I'm judgmental but because I don't trust myself to handle that kind of situation in a way that'll keep you safe. I'm just not experienced in that manner is all, and I'm not confident I'd be able to keep you safe."

"Caleb Eckhart, what kind of girl do you think I am?" she asks, batting her eyelashes.

"What I think, Amber Watson, is that with me, you're allowed to be any kind of girl you want."

The expression on her face is the one he wanted to see because he smiles warm, sinks further down into the tub, his big toe finding and then gently grazing her nub.

She picks up the pen, but the sight of the empty page terrifies her.

"Maybe if it wasn't the stationary for my *mother's* hotel."

"Come on now," he says gently, and just then his big toe finds her clit and begins rubbing lazy, gentle circles around it. "Just turn the paper over if it bothers you."

His voice is something between a growl and a purr. Between its lustful timber and the job he's doing on her under the water, she can barely see straight enough to keep the pen steady.

"Do you want me to stop?" he asks.

"My writing assignment or your big toe?"

"Either? Both?"

"Just promise me something."

"Sure."

"I don't want you doing it if it's not something you want to do," she says.

He nods solemnly, but she can tell he's sure there's not a chance in hell he won't want to do it, no matter what it is.

"You promise me?" she asks.

"I promise," he says.

"Okay," she says. "Now quit it with your foot so I can concentrate."

He jerks his foot back so suddenly it sloshes the water in the tub, which causes both of them to crack up for several minutes. Once they manage to calm down, once she takes a deep breath and finds herself staring again at the blank, empty page, she finds the courage to say, "Why is this so important to you, Caleb?"

"Because after what you went through with songbird, I don't want you to be afraid to ask me for anything."

And just like that, she's writing. She's writing without regard for how he'll react when he reads it. The fantasy isn't really all that outlandish or kinky. Girlfriends of hers have shared far stranger ones with her over cocktails. But this one involves dark woods, woods as dark as the ones Caleb got lost in on that long ago night. True, it also involves being found. Hard. Still, it seems like a cruel trick of fate, the fact that her most private, unrealized sexual fantasy could trigger one of Caleb's most painful memories. But maybe she's overthinking it.

By the time she's done, she's filled two pages with her hurried block printing.

Her heart hammering, she slides the coffee table book and the pages back across the edge of the tub toward Caleb, who dabs his hands dry on a nearby towel and picks up the pages gently and carefully, as if they were made of old, thin parchment.

She watches his face as he reads, watches the tense set of his jaw, the focus apparent in his dazzling blue eyes. Watches him suck in a deep breath through his nostrils when he gets to a certain line—she has no idea which one, but she's got a few guesses. Is it stirring painful memories for him or something else?

Look down and see, genius, she realizes.

The head of his majestic, swollen cock just pierces the water's surface.

"Oh, Amber," he growls, still reading. "Amber Louise Watson."

It's been forever since anyone's used her middle name. This must be serious.

"What?" she asks.

He sets the pages aside.

"Get ready, baby," he says. "We are *so* doing this!"

13

Are we really going to do this?

Amber's lost count of how many times she's asked herself this question in the past thirty minutes. It would have made more sense to ask Caleb back when they were still plotting out the details. But she's on her own now, making her way through the woods just below the cottage, bound for the spot Caleb marked on the map Nora left in their room.

When she'd asked him how he'd ensure their privacy, he'd told her not to worry, that he'd take care of that part. That he'd take care of everything. All she had to do was trust him.

They'd agreed on two safe words. Slow down was *leaf;* full stop was *Chevron.* But still, the thought of him asking Nora or—oh, dear Lord, no—her mother to keep one of the hiking trials clear just so the two of them could do some outdoor role-play leaves her flush with shame.

The wrong kind of shame.

Of course, he'd probably try some sort of cover story. But it wouldn't matter, because neither Nora nor her mother would believe it for a second.

Her flashlight beam bounces across the old, capped wellhead he marked on the map. Rustic benches sit on either side. A dense canopy of interlocking oak branches filters the night sky above. If she keeps walking, she'll hit woods too dense to move through without a machete. Now she realizes why Caleb picked this particular location. It's the dead end of a hiking trail, a long distance from the inn's main building, but closer to their cottage if things go wrong.

She's here. She's got everything she needs—the blanket, the box of condoms, the flashlight, and the T-shirt they've already tested out on her wrists. She can turn the shirt into a makeshift pair of cotton handcuffs, easy to escape if she gets cold feet, just tight enough to give the illusion she's actually restrained.

She spreads the blanket out in front of her, parallel to one side of the bench and its curved metal armrest.

This is the part of the script about which she's the most nervous.

Once she turns the flashlight beam off, she's got ten minutes.

Once she turns the flashlight beam off, she's committed.

Unless, of course, she decides to use one of her safe words once they've started. But the ten things she has to do before the scenario starts—that's what they've agreed to call it, apparently. The scenario!—those have to be perfect! Otherwise, the whole thing will turn into either a colossal joke or a huge embarrassment. Or both.

God save me, she prays silently. *Save me from feeling like an idiot. The other stuff? I might be beyond hope in that regard.*

She kills the flashlight.

She slides out of her panties and kicks them to one side.

She drops to her knees on the blanket, and then, just as she practiced back in the cabin, she laces the T-shirt around the bench's armrest until she's tied it loosely around her hands. She tugs gently with both wrists until the cotton's tight enough to give the illusion she's handcuffed.

Then she waits.

She waits as the cool night air kisses the cheeks of her ass and everything in between.

She waits as the fear—of wildlife, of discovery, of mortification—turns into a feeling of exhilaration. A feeling of taking all of the rules and limitations and lectures she's endured all her life, all the finger-wagging nonsense abut what good girls are and what good girls have to do, and blowing them into the air like they were nothing but a handful of sand.

Footsteps approach, cracking twigs. Fast at first, then slower. Then Caleb lets out a long, slow whistle.

"Well, well, well, well, *wellllll,*" Caleb says. Only for now, he's not Caleb. He's just some random cowboy who emerged from the dark woods to find her half naked and tied to a bench. And he's playing up the accent too, just like she asked. "What have we *here?* Lord!"

"Sir, could you untie me please?" she asks.

Her voice sounds like someone else's. She's speaking words she's imagined countless times while pleasuring herself with a showerhead or her fingers, all while her husband slept in the other room. Or lied to her about staying late at work so he could bang his mistress.

"Untie you?" he asks, feigning shock. "Are you tied up, ma'am? Is that what you are?" He reaches down and tugs at the makeshift handcuffs. Pretends as if they're locked in place. "Well, you most certainly are, aren't you? Now how in the heck did a pretty little thing like you get tied up out here in these dark woods?"

"It was my husband..."

"Your *husband* did this?"

"Yes and then he left me here. We were playing a game and he freaked out and he left me."

"A game, huh? What kind of game? The kind of game where you gotta turn this pretty ass to the woods?" A light touch. Feather light. Torture light. Just a graze of his finger from the very top of the crack of her ass up into the small of her back.

Oh, God, he's good at this. He's. So. Damn. Good. At—

"And, uh, whose idea was this little game?" he asks.

"Mine," she answers, sounding as sheepish as she can. Which isn't all that hard. Because she's in this, gripped by it. Feeling the boundaries between the scene and reality blur into a kind of blinding heat.

"I see. So it wasn't your husband's idea?"

"No. He said he was into it, but he freaked out. And he called me all kinds of names and ran away."

"Really?" There's concern in his voice now, and a bit of protective anger. "What kind of names?"

"He said I was disgusting. He called me a filthy, dirty whore."

"And then he just left you?"

"Yes, sir. He just left me."

"With no way to get free," he says as if he's realizing the implications of this for the first time. The implications for *him*.

She hasn't looked at him once since he crouched down next to her. She knows if she looks at him, her juices will start to flow. And it's way too soon for her to do or say or look at the things that will induce a moist inclination toward surrender. That's his job. If he follows the script. If he plays his part.

So far, he's doing an Oscar-worthy job.

"Sir," she whispers. "Please. If you could just untie me so I can get home to my husband."

"So why are you in such a rush to get home to your husband when he called you all those rotten names and left you out here in the woods all by yourself?"

"I just... Please, sir."

"Yeah. I don't know."

"Don't know what, sir?"

"Well, it just doesn't make much sense, is all."

"What doesn't make sense, sir?"

He traces several fingers along the crack of her ass, then down, ever so lightly across her mound. A quick, furtive, stolen motion that still manages to touch the most intimate part of her. "When you find a pretty little pussy like this out in the woods, you don't just take it straight home," he growls.

Home run, she thinks. *Home fucking run.* They've been improvising the rest of the dialogue but this is the exact line she wrote out for him earlier that night, the line that's electrified her fantasies for years. A line that makes her feel both degraded and celebrated, captured and set free. And his tone, his delivery. Both were perfect! But all she says is, "Sir, please. You have to take me home."

Or fuck me. Right here. Right now. I can't wait.

"Tell you what, little lady. I'll make a deal with you."

"Okay," she manages.

"You're gonna let me put my hands all over this body of yours. And if that pussy of yours stays dry, or if those cute little nipples stay soft under my fingertips, I'll take you home to your husband. But if you're a dirty slut just like your husband says, and you get all hot just from the feel of my touch, well, then, honey, I'm going to fuck you right out here in these woods. Does that sound like a deal?"

"Yes, sir. On one condition."

"What's that?"

"You can't touch my…"

"Your what, honey?"

"My clit, sir."

"Okay. Sounds fair. I won't touch your pretty clit, but I'll touch the rest of you. Every last inch of you. Does that sound fair?"

"Yes, sir. But only with your fingers."

"Well, alright, then," he says, lips to her ear. "Sounds like a deal. Let's get started."

He sinks down onto the blanket behind her, the denim of his jeans scratching the skin of her ass. He reaches around her and under her T-shirt, cups her bare breasts as if the sheer weight of them were a pleasure in and of itself. Grazes her nipples with his fingers.

"Bet you want to lose, don't you, little lady?" he rasps into her ear. "Maybe if I win, I won't fuck you out here. Maybe I'll take you back to my cabin. With my buddies."

"Buddies?"

"Yeah. Maybe I'll take you back to my cabin and me and my buddies will take turns on you."

Yeah, uhm, I didn't write a word about your buddies.

"Leaf."

"Maybe I'll take you back to my cabin and make my buddies watch while I have my way with you."

Much better.

"Whatever you say, sir."

"That's right. If I win, you do *whatever* I say. That's the deal."

He bends forward so he can dip one hand all the way down to her mound. He keeps his word, avoiding her clit, running his fingers gently down her folds instead.

"I don't know, honey," he drawls. "Feeling pretty hot down here."

"Is it?"

"Yeah. Sure is. Now we made a deal, isn't that right, honey?"

He's using his palm now, rubbing it across her folds, back and forth, stopping just shy of her swollen, aching nub. Teasing it so well she's aching for him to touch it.

"Yes, sir. We made a deal."

"So if I free these hands of yours, you're not gonna try to run away on me now, are you?"

"No, sir. I'm not going to try to run."

"Good." He rips the T-shirt away from the bench's armrest. "Because I'm going to have to examine you up close now to see how you're responding to my little test here."

Suddenly she's on her back and he's lying on the blanket beside her. He's pulled her T-shirt up and over her breasts. Now she feels even more exposed to the night, to *him*. And this time, when his fingers pass over her folds, there's no ignoring the wetness there, even though she'd like him to. Even thought she'd love to draw out this teasing for another hour. Hours, even.

"Oh," he says with a start. "Oh, my. You've got a wet pussy here, girl."

"Do I?"

"Yes, ma'am. A nice, hot, wet pussy. For the life of me, I just can't figure out how a man would leave a pussy this hot and wet all the way out here in these woods. But I guess I shouldn't complain. Because now it's all mine. Ain't that right, little lady?"

His desire for her, real and authentic and unscripted, makes his voice shake. She stares up at him for the first time since they started. He's got his Stetson on and his light leather jacket and his Levi's. Being practically stark naked and under his control while he's still fully dressed only makes her hotter and wetter.

"And since we had a deal," he says as he tugs her T-shirt up over her head. "It looks like it's time to pay up."

He fingers the box of condoms she dropped on the blanket when she first got there.

"I've got your husband to thank for a lot of things, don't I?" he says, then tears the condom wrapper open with his teeth.

"How about you stop talking about my husband and take what's yours?"

"Yeah," he says, sliding out of his jacket and unbuttoning his plaid shirt. "Well, he was right about one thing."

He unbuttons his jeans, frees his cock, slides the condom on with one hand. His tone is calm and collected but his speed is all horny, desperate teenager. The combination of the two makes her feel as if she's the one who's got him under control, not the other way around.

"You really are a filthy little girl," he growls.

He closes one hand gently around her throat. With the other, he drags the head of his cock back and forth over her folds, then in a slow circle over her clit.

He's free to touch it now that she lost.

Won. I won. I so won.

"But right now, you're *my* filthy little girl."

Slowly, he pushes inside her. As he drives himself deeper, his lips hover inches above hers. There's wonder in his expression, the joy at being inside of her for the first time. Not inside the character she was playing seconds before. Inside of her. Amber Watson.

He's so big. So much bigger than any man she's been with. But he's taking his time, thank God. Kissing her neck the way he did in her front hallway the night before. Palming her breasts the way he did in the motel room that morning. It's like his desire demands that he tend to every inch of her in any way he can. Stroking, teasing, tasting, gazing.

He's also dropping the role, becoming himself once again now that they're joined in a way they've never been before.

"You like that?" he rasps. "You like getting fucked by a stranger in the woods?"

She wraps her legs around his waist and squeezes. His eyes pop open.

He seems unsure of what she's doing until she starts to sit up. This gives him no choice but to rock backward onto his haunches under her shifting weight. She's still impaled, but sitting up now, clutching the sides of his face in her hands.

"You're not a stranger, not anymore," she says, even though they never planned to drop the fantasy like this. "You're Caleb." She kisses his cheek, the line of his jaw. "Be Caleb." She pulls back, grips his face again. "Fuck me like Caleb wants to fuck me. Like you've always wanted to fuck me."

A groan escapes him, the sound of the role dropping away, the sound of the man who's wanted her for years melting into her, driving himself into her, tasting her nipples as he thrusts with his powerful hips. His Stetson slides off the back of his head and thuds softly to the blanket behind him. The cool night kisses her everywhere now, except in those spots where the heat from his hands and his lips and his powerful arms set her skin aflame.

"Amber." It's a plea, full of equal parts pleasure and resistance.

"Yes, baby."

"Amber...I..."

"Yes."

She grabs the side of his face. His thrusts intensify. His eyes shoot open as he stares up into hers. There's that plea again. He's seeking permission to let loose inside of her. "Anything," he gasps. "I will be *anything* for you."

"Be the man who comes inside me," she whispers.

That does it.

His jaw goes slack, his mouth a near perfect *O*. The waves of his climax pulse through his hard, powerful body as he drives himself deep inside her with a frenzy of hard thrusts. His bellows become shudders. He wraps his arms around her, holding her against him as tightly as he can, which in their current position, places his face just above her breasts.

Well, I got mine last night, I guess, she thinks.

Suddenly, he tilts her backward, one arm curved around her lower back for support.

Once he's laid her down on the blanket, he reaches down, grips the base of the condom and pulls himself gently from her folds.

As he kneads and massages her thighs, his fingers drive waves of pleasure up into her sex. Before Caleb, every man she'd been with had rolled off her as soon as he'd peaked. Now, without pausing to free himself from his condom, he goes to work on her with his tongue. It's slow and languid but also perfect. Not the divine oral assault he'd subjected her to that morning. Something different and more careful. Having come allows him to pursue her pleasure in an unhurried way.

"Waited so long for this," he whispers. "Waited so damn long for you, for this."

In the past, her orgasms have been long, slow builds. Sometimes too long and too slow. This one comes on sudden as lightning, triggered by the power of his tongue and his whispers working in tandem. She grips the back of his head. Pleasure curls her toes and makes her hips feel liquid. He refuses to release her clit from his sucking lips even as she lets out gasping, stuttering cries. She bucks against him, fights the urge to flail her limbs, and still he doesn't relent.

She's not sure which way is up or down until he settles down next to her and takes her in his strong arms.

It takes her a while to remember how to breathe.

"Well," he finally says, lifting his head up off the blanket so he can look into her eyes. "How'd I do?" he asks with a broad, goofy grin.

"Damn," she whispers.

"You only had to use the safe word once. Pretty successful, if you ask me."

"Yeah, and it was the *light* safe word. Not the, you know, red alert."

"True."

"You don't really want to share me with your buddies, do you?"

"I'd sooner rip their damn faces off. Forgive me. I'd never acted before. I got kinda carried away."

"Okay. Good."

"I mean, I was just trying anything 'cause I couldn't wait for you to get wet. Hell, I would have put on a goddamn Kermit the Frog costume if I'd thought it—"

"Okay, okay. That's enough. Thank you."

"Seriously, though. Were you happy with my performance?"

"Baby, happy's not the word."

"Good." He kisses her gently on the tip of her nose. "I like it when you call me baby."

"Do you? I'll call you baby anytime you want."

"Good. Do it again."

"Baby," she whispers.

"Now do it while you give me a kiss," he whispers.

"Baby," she whispers and kisses him on the cheek.

"Awesome. Now do it while you lick my balls."

"*Shut up, jackass!*" she cries through her uncontrollable laughter.

He's laughing as hard as she is. When she goes to slap him across his chest, he grabs for her hand and the ensuing tussle lands them in a new position, spooning like lovers snuggled up together in bed.

"I guess we'll have to do one of your fantasies soon," she says. "It's only fair, right?"

"Aw, you don't have to worry about me." Her back is to him, but she can hear him trying to suppress a smile. "I'm easy. My biggest turn-ons are wine and conversation."

"Are you always a sass mouth after you get laid?"

"Also, stuffed animals. Love me some stuffed animals."

"Alright, well, I'll make a note of that."

"Seriously, though. I don't have any big fantasies."

"Interesting. I'll remember that."

"Although…"

"Oh, boy. Here we go. What's it gonna be? French maid or schoolgirl?"

"Well, I was gonna say now's a terrible time to ask me this question."

"Why's that?"

"Because I can't think of a better fantasy than being with you now, just like this."

She rolls over so she can see his expression. He's not being sarcastic, not in the slightest. In fact, he looks a little nervous to have answered so directly.

"Do you have any idea what you did for me tonight?" she asks. "Do you have any idea the shame you lifted from me, from my body, from my heart? And the fact that you were the one doing it, the man I've always wanted. The man I've always loved…I mean, I can't even…"

"Of course I do, darlin'. Why do you think I did it?"

She snuggles up against his chest because for some crazy reason, it feels like this position will allow her to hold his words more closely to her heart.

After a while he says, "I do kinda have a thing for librarians, though."

"Good," she answers. "That's an easy costume."

14

The Haven Creek Inn only serves breakfast and dinner, so when Amber and Caleb walk into the dining hall at half past noon, they've got the place all to themselves. Except for her mom, who's setting one of the corner tables just for them.

The chandeliers are made out of antlers, a long painting on one wall replicates the view outside, and there's a wall of glass doors looking out over a stone patio and the steps leading down to the swimming pool. All told, the building's big enough to accommodate a wedding party of around one hundred people, more if you open all the doors.

When her mother sees them, she sets down her water pitcher and gives them a warm smile.

"And how are we today this *very* late morning, Mister Watson and Miss…" She remembers they already have the same last name and coughs to hide her embarrassment.

"Don't worry, Momma. He's getting a lawyer when we get back to Dallas so he can change his last name back to Eckhart."

"Oh," her mother says. "Okay."

A strange blend of emotions, most of them dark, it looks like, passes through her mother's stare.

Caught, her mom looks away and gestures for them to sit.

"I'll go see if your pancakes are ready."

"What was that about?" Amber asks.

"The name thing's kinda weird for now. Don't worry. I'll fix it."

A few minutes later, her mother's back, a plate in each hand. Lemon ricotta pancakes, served on the inn's signature blue toile china, pads of butter sliding off them like skiers in melting snow. Too bad her mother's refusing to look either one of them in the eye.

"Momma, what?"

"Nothing. Y'all enjoy your pancakes."

She turns to leave.

"Momma!"

Amber points to the empty chair. Her mother flounces down into it. It's Caleb to whom she suddenly gives her full attention.

"I want this trip to be special for you both, I really do. And I hate to mention anything that touches upon that *jerk*. But what you said just now, Caleb, about changing your name?"

"Yes, ma'am," he answers.

"I don't have a problem with it. I really don't. But...these things with the trust and the bar..."

Amber's heart drops. Her cheeks flame.

Why didn't she think of this before?

"You and Abel," her mother continues, "y'all made all these arrangements that Amber and I didn't know anything about. And according to what she told me the other day on the phone, they're our first line of defense against Joel if he tries to make trouble in the LLC. So tell me, if you go changing your name right now, I mean, before we get this all sorted out. Is that gonna cause problems for Watson's? For everyone who works there?"

"Oh my God," Amber whispers.

"Oh, honey, don't get upset. It's just a technicality. But maybe for a little while, until we get Joel out of the picture, nobody changes their names, okay? And I hate to say it, but that also means nobody nullifies any adoptions either."

"It's fine," Amber finally manages. But her performance is a lousy one, so she tries again. "We'll figure it out. It's fine. Let's just eat." *Second verse, wore than the first*, she thinks. Because it's more than a name, and it's more than a piece of paper and they all know it, and that's why the three of them just sit for a while.

"It's not fine," Caleb says.

When she looks up at him, he doesn't seem angry, just calm and resolute.

"And it's not a problem," he says.

"What do you mean?" her mother asks.

"The trust documents don't list me as his heir. Yeah, I'm the trustee, but as an individual, not a family member. A simple name change won't affect that as long as it's properly filed. And nothing about the documents we drew up stipulates that a family member has to be the trustee."

"Really?" her mother says, stunned. "Abel agreed to that?"

"Not at first. But I managed to sell him on it."

"How?" her mother asks.

"I told him if this was really going to be a fail-safe in case Joel turned out to make a mess of Watson's, he should keep it as separate from family as possible. He thought I was worrying about a technicality and I pointed out that putting language in there about me being his son was just about emotions, not the law. As long as I was named as the trustee, I'd be able to keep tabs on Joel and shut down his promotions budget if I so chose. Didn't matter whether I was Abel's son or some guy he just met on the street. Unless I went and nullified the adoption, what did it matter whether or not the documents listed me as an heir?"

"And that's what you really wanted, wasn't it?" her mother asks. "The option to nullify the adoption at some point."

Caleb tightens his grip on Amber's hand. "Guess so. I've never been big on hope before these past few days. But I guess I had a shred of it in me back then."

"And what did he say?" Amber asks. "What did he say when you asked him to just list you by name and not as his son?"

"Not much. He was pretty sick by then and we were rushing to put the documents together while we still had time. I remember he just shook his head and kinda laughed and said some old saying that I'd never heard him say before."

"What old saying?" her mother asks, sitting forward suddenly, her voice tight as a drawstring.

"I think he said... Sometimes the road rises up to meet you instead of beat you."

Her mother's hands fly to her mouth.

Amber hears herself suck in a breath, and then suddenly she's blinking back tears.

"He knew," her mother whispers. "He knew what you really wanted."

"What do you mean?" he asks.

"It wasn't just an old saying," Amber manages. "He used to say it all the time but he stopped the night your parents died 'cause he thought it would be insensitive given how they'd died. He always said it when he didn't get his way."

"No," her mother says, shaking her head. "It was more than that. He first heard it in the Marines. He didn't just say it when he didn't get his way. He said it when he'd lost a battle of some sort. Something big. Something he'd been working on for years. Something like keeping you two apart."

"Oh, Momma," Amber says.

"He knew," her mother says through tears. "He knew why you wanted the trust written that way and he didn't stop you."

As she rises to her feet, her mother holds out one hand as if her tears are something outside of herself she can literally hold at bay. But the best she can manage is to turn herself toward the glass doors, her back to them as she cries into her hands.

Once she catches her breath, she finally says, "Goddamn, but that man could be a stubborn son of a gun. But every now and then he knew how to lose with grace."

Amber rises, takes her mother in her arms. They stare out at the sunlit treetops and the piled high clouds blowing across the blue sky.

"But I miss that bullheaded bastard, I really do," her mother finally says.

"Me too," Amber answers.

Clearing her throat, her mother turns quickly and kisses Amber on the forehead.

As she stands over Caleb, one hand resting on his shoulder as if she were anointing him with a new title, her mother says. "Promise me you'll change your name back as soon as you get to Dallas, Caleb. Promise me you'll walk right through the door Abel left open for you. Then we'll be the family we were truly meant to be."

She bends down and kisses him on the forehead too.

"Now eat your pancakes before they get cold."

Amber watches her mother hurry from the room.

"Should I follow her?" she asks Caleb. "I feel like I should follow her."

"I think when your mother wants your attention she knows how to get it."

"That's right, I guess."

He pats her empty chair with his hand. But it's his mouthful of delicious, molten pancake that really convinces her to take a seat. Once she does, and once he's managed to swallow, he raises his water glass.

"Bad luck to toast with water," she says.

"Fine," he says and picks up one of the tiny flower vases studded with sprigs of lavender. He clears his throat until she picks up one of the other ones in kind. "A toast."

"To who?"

"To *those birds!* Who do you think?"

"Alright, easy, cowboy. It's been an emotional morning."

"Fine," he says, then he clears his throat, lowers and then raises the lavender again as if he's rebooting. "A toast."

"A toast," she says. "With lavender."

"And sass, as is to be expected with the two of us."

"Indeed. What are we toasting?"

"Well, I can only speak for myself. I'm saying good-bye to the sister I never wanted and hello to the woman I've always loved."

"And I'm saying, I love you too. But you knew that already."

"It's nice to be reminded."

"Don't worry. I'll never let you forget it."

Epilogue

"Given that I'm losing my favorite assistant, I'm not really sure why I should consider this a celebration," Belinda Baxter says, then she scoops a handful of beer nuts into her mouth and chews angrily while surveying the crowd inside Watson's.

The bar's as packed as Amber's ever seen it, the kind of turnout they usually see for a concert or a record release party for some band that's gone gold. But this is a private event. For the most part, the guests are employees, both present and former, their friends and family, and pretty much every living relative Amber has in the states of Texas, Oklahoma, and Louisiana.

And they're all celebrating one simple fact. Just that afternoon, Joel Claire sold his majority stake in the LLC that owns Watson's back to Amber and her mother, and in turn, she and her mother signed over a majority share to the bar's new owner, Caleb Eckhart.

Belinda, on the other hand, has decided to turn tonight's festivities into a wake for her favorite personal assistant.

"I'm sorry you're choosing to see only the darkness, Belinda," Amber says. "But if I remember correctly, when I first told you I was going to take over the books for this place, you had a much different reaction."

"I don't know what you're talking about, miss."

"I believe you said something along the lines of, 'If I had a boyfriend that hot, I'd be riding him everyday at work too.'"

"That may be true, but you should still allow me my feelings. It's only fair. You know I had to hire two women and a gay guy to replace you. And the gay guy didn't even look twice at my shoe collection. He wants to work with my *cars*. I swear, I never should have encouraged you to look out for your best interests."

Her former employer's glass of Merlot looks distinctly out of place amidst the beer bottles and rock glasses scattered along the rest of the bar. But at least Belinda's made an attempt to dress for the venue. She's wearing a shiny jacket with Western tassels. Puffy and shiny and not exactly cowgirl material and…are those entwined C's on the lapel, almost hidden by a jeweled broach shaped like a horseshoe?

"I didn't know Chanel made anything with Western fringe," Amber says.

"They don't. I had one of my new girls add it this morning."

Just then, Belinda's face falls. She fortifies herself with a quick slug of wine.

Amber follows the direction of Belinda's gaze to…her *mother?* Really? What on earth does Belinda have against her mother? Is she still embarrassed by all that Desire Exchange silliness? It's not possible. The two women have been in the same room several times since then and neither has said a word about it.

Is it Nora? She's walking right next to her mom, wearing one of those thousand-watt smiles, and maybe, Amber wonders, trying to scope out any alien/human hybrid children who might be hiding among the attendees?

It's Amanda Crawford!

The woman's dressed in a flowy cocktail dress that screams, *I'm too rich to be here!* She's also wearing a stony, furious expression that matches Belinda's. The closer they get, the more Amanda raises her Louis Vuitton purse in front of her as if it were a shield meant to withstand both bullets, knives, and the furious glares of women like Belinda. So far, her mom and Nora are oblivious to the currents of icy tension passing between the two overdressed multimillionaires.

Nora gives Amber a huge hug. But her mother just gives her a perfunctory kiss on the cheek. The two of them spent most of the day together in lawyer's offices finalizing the paperwork of her ex-husband's departure from the business. And that's good. Because Amber doesn't want to be bothered with a lot of greetings right now. She wants to know why Belinda and Amanda are staring at each other like cornered rattlers.

"So I take it you two know each other?" Amber finally says.

"We do," Belinda says.

"Indeed," Amanda says. "We do."

"It's nice to see you standing up, Amanda," Belinda says.

"Oh. Don't be silly. You're just enjoying one of those rare moments of seeing someone other than yourself."

"Oh, dear," Nora says under her breath.

"Uhm," her mother says. "Should we, maybe, clear the air here? Is something going on that we don't know about?"

"All the ceiling fans in the world couldn't clear the air when *this* one's in the room," Belinda snarls, then she takes her wine glass and departs into the crowd.

"Whoa," Amber says.

"I'm sorry," Amanda says. "Was some creature just speaking or did one of you have Mexican for lunch?"

And then Amanda's gone too.

"What on Earth was *that?*" her mother cries.

"I have no idea," Amber says.

"Well, I think they're upset with each other for some reason and they don't want to say why," Nora says.

"You think, Nora?" her mother answers. "Get yourself a beer. I'm driving."

Amber's mother takes Belinda's suddenly empty barstool.

Nora heads off to get the attention of one of the overworked bartenders.

"If I never talk to another lawyer again, it'll be too soon," her mother says.

"I second that," Amber says. "But we did it. That's all that matters. We did it."

"You can say that again," her mother says.

"I will. A whole bunch."

"Also, I've got a present for you, sweetie," her mother says. But she's scanning the crowd, not reaching into her purse or revealing some gift bag she might have been hiding behind her back.

"I'm ready," she says.

"An old friend of mine from Baylor knows little Mary's aunt."

"Wait. *Mary* Mary?"

"Yes, Joel's Mary. Well, it turns out she's not Joel's Mary anymore. She already jumped ship for the drummer in some band that can actually get a gig. Joel apparently did a whole night of singing sad karaoke at some bar in Irving before they kicked him out."

"Well, God bless 'em," Amber says, toasting the air in front of her with her beer bottle. "God bless 'em both."

One of the bands they've hired for the evening has been tuning up on stage for the last several minutes. But it's Caleb who now takes the microphone. He clears his throat a few times.

"Alright, everyone. If I could just have your attention."

There's some whoops and applause from the crowd, but he quiets them with a wave of his hand.

"Now, I'm not sure if all y'all heard but as of today, Watson's is under new management."

The reaction inside is touchdown-at-a-Cowboys-game loud. And it goes on for several minutes as people clap and scream and war whoop.

"Wow," Amber cries to her mother. "They really hated Joel."

"Or they just love Caleb as much as you do," her mother shouts back.

When the applause and the screaming finally die down, Caleb's got a big smile on his face, but all he does is nod his head and touch the brim of his hat as if someone complimented him on his jeans. "Thank you. I appreciate it. And I can guarantee you, we're gonna keep this place on track so it lasts another twenty-five, or hell, let's make it *fifty* years being just the kind of place Abel Watson intended it to be."

More applause. And then people start shouting other intervals of time. One hundred years, three hundred. It's like a badly organized auction before Caleb silences it with a winning grin and an outstretched arm.

"Now, some of you may know my history with the Watson family is a long one. And if it hadn't been for them, I'm not quite sure where I would have ended up. Certainly not here with all you fine people, making my head swell with all your rowdiness and attention. But I did something else this week. Something important. And I need to tell y'all about it, regardless of what you're gonna think or what your opinions may be.

"See, a long time ago my parents died, and Abel Watson decided the best way he could take care of me was if he welcomed me into his family. So he adopted me. And that adoption probably saved my life. Today, though, things are a little bit different. You see, years ago... Well, let me put it this way. You ever know the minute you lay eyes on someone that they're the one for you? I mean, you ever hear someone's voice and think, that's the voice I want to wake up to for the rest of my life even if she's yelling at my lazy ass to get out of bed and get to work."

Peals of laughter and a few whoops of agreement come up from the crowd. But Amber's heart is in her throat as he continues. This is the moment she's feared almost as much as losing him—the moment when they stop ducking questions about whether or not their relationship has changed.

She expected him to make some sort of speech, and they'd agreed that tonight they'd stop hiding. But she's not sure if she's ready for him to be this specific and detailed. At least not in front of this many people. People who might already be judging them silently; people who will now have the chance to judge them out loud.

"Well, that's how I felt the first time I laid eyes on Amber Watson," he says.

The roar that comes up from the crowd is almost as loud as the one that greeted his announcement Watson's was under new management. And just like that, all her feelings of anxiety lift, carried away by the full-voiced joy and support of people who've only wanted the best for her.

He waits for it to die down again, then he says, "So, when I tell you that I went and had my adoption nullified, it's not because Abel Watson wasn't a good man and it's not because the Watsons aren't the most important people in my life and always will be. It's because years ago, before my parents died and before Abel took me in, Amber and I realized we were fated to be something else for each other. And every day since then, we've just been delaying the inevitable. And that's why I'd like to remind her that I love her. That's why I'd like me and her to be the first official dance of the new Watson's."

"Wipe your face, honey," her mother says.

"What?" Amber says. "I didn't wear any makeup 'cause I knew he'd do this."

Her mother reaches into her purse and hands her a tissue. Amber walks through the crowd, cheering faces on all sides of her, and then, once she's a few feet away, Caleb jumps off the edge of the stage and lands on the dance floor, arm out, ready to take her for a spin.

"Toldja I'd give you this dance, Amber Watson," he says once she's close enough to hear him.

"You sure did, Caleb Eckhart. You sure did."

"You ready, baby."

"So ready," she says.

He takes her outstretched hand and grips her waist. She panics for a moment when she realizes she doesn't know if they're about to waltz or two-step or what. But once the music starts none of that matters. The only dance that matters is one she does with him.

* * * *

Also from 1001 Dark Nights and Christopher Rice, discover The Flame, The Surrender Gate, Kiss the Flame, and Desire & Ice.

Sign up for the 1001 Dark Nights Newsletter
and be entered to win a Tiffany Key necklace.

There's a contest every month!

Go to www.1001DarkNights.com to subscribe.

As a bonus, all subscribers will receive a free
1001 Dark Nights story
The First Night
by Lexi Blake & M.J. Rose

Turn the page for a full list of the
1001 Dark Nights fabulous novellas...

Discover 1001 Dark Nights Collection Three

HIDDEN INK by Carrie Ann Ryan
A Montgomery Ink Novella

BLOOD ON THE BAYOU by Heather Graham
A Cafferty & Quinn Novella

SEARCHING FOR MINE by Jennifer Probst
A Searching For Novella

DANCE OF DESIRE by Christopher Rice

ROUGH RHYTHM by Tessa Bailey
A Made In Jersey Novella

DEVOTED by Lexi Blake
A Masters and Mercenaries Novella

Z by Larissa Ione
A Demonica Underworld Novella

FALLING UNDER YOU by Laurelin Paige
A Fixed Trilogy Novella

EASY FOR KEEPS by Kristen Proby
A Boudreaux Novella

UNCHAINED by Elisabeth Naughton
An Eternal Guardians Novella

HARD TO SERVE by Laura Kaye
A Hard Ink Novella

DRAGON FEVER by Donna Grant
A Dark Kings Novella

KAYDEN/SIMON by Alexandra Ivy/Laura Wright
A Bayou Heat Novella

STRUNG UP by Lorelei James
A Blacktop Cowboys® Novella

MIDNIGHT UNTAMED by Lara Adrian
A Midnight Breed Novella

TRICKED by Rebecca Zanetti
A Dark Protectors Novella

DIRTY WICKED by Shayla Black
A Wicked Lovers Novella

A SEDUCTIVE INVITATION by Lauren Blakely
A Seductive Nights New York Novella

SWEET SURRENDER by Liliana Hart
A MacKenzie Family Novella

For more information visit www.1001DarkNights.com.

Discover 1001 Dark Nights Collection One

FOREVER WICKED by Shayla Black
CRIMSON TWILIGHT by Heather Graham
CAPTURED IN SURRENDER by Liliana Hart
SILENT BITE: A SCANGUARDS WEDDING by Tina Folsom
DUNGEON GAMES by Lexi Blake
AZAGOTH by Larissa Ione
NEED YOU NOW by Lisa Renee Jones
SHOW ME, BABY by Cherise Sinclair
ROPED IN by Lorelei James
TEMPTED BY MIDNIGHT by Lara Adrian
THE FLAME by Christopher Rice
CARESS OF DARKNESS by Julie Kenner

Also from 1001 Dark Nights
TAME ME by J. Kenner

For more information visit www.1001DarkNights.com.

Discover 1001 Dark Nights Collection Two

WICKED WOLF by Carrie Ann Ryan
WHEN IRISH EYES ARE HAUNTING by Heather Graham
EASY WITH YOU by Kristen Proby
MASTER OF FREEDOM by Cherise Sinclair
CARESS OF PLEASURE by Julie Kenner
ADORED by Lexi Blake
HADES by Larissa Ione
RAVAGED by Elisabeth Naughton
DREAM OF YOU by Jennifer L. Armentrout
STRIPPED DOWN by Lorelei James
RAGE/KILLIAN by Alexandra Ivy/Laura Wright
DRAGON KING by Donna Grant
PURE WICKED by Shayla Black
HARD AS STEEL by Laura Kaye
STROKE OF MIDNIGHT by Lara Adrian
ALL HALLOWS EVE by Heather Graham
KISS THE FLAME by Christopher Rice
DARING HER LOVE by Melissa Foster
TEASED by Rebecca Zanetti
THE PROMISE OF SURRENDER by Liliana Hart

Also from 1001 Dark Nights
THE SURRENDER GATE By Christopher Rice
SERVICING THE TARGET By Cherise Sinclair

For more information visit www.1001DarkNights.com.

About Christopher Rice

New York Times bestselling author Christopher Rice's first foray into erotic romance, THE FLAME, earned accolades from some of the genre's most beloved authors. "Sensual, passionate and intelligent," wrote Lexi Blake, "it's everything an erotic romance should be." J. Kenner called it "absolutely delicious," Cherise Sinclair hailed it as "beautifully lyrical" and Lorelei James announced, "I look forward to reading more!" He went on to publish two more installments in The Desire Exchange Series, THE SURRENDER GATE and KISS THE FLAME. Prior to his erotic romance debut, Christopher published four New York Times bestselling thrillers before the age of 30, received a Lambda Literary Award and was declared one of People Magazine's Sexiest Men Alive. His supernatural thrillers, THE HEAVENS RISE and THE VINES, were both nominated for Bram Stoker Awards. Aside from authoring eight works of dark suspense, Christopher is also the co-host and executive producer of THE DINNER PARTY SHOW WITH CHRISTOPHER RICE & ERIC SHAW QUINN, all the episodes of which can be downloaded and streamed at www.TheDinnerPartyShow.com and from iTunes. Subscribe to The Dinner Party Show's You Tube channel to receive the newest content.

Desire & Ice
A MacKenzie Family Novella
By Christopher Rice
Now Available

I'm so thrilled and grateful New York Times bestseller Liliana Hart allowed me to reference characters from her MacKenzie Family stories here in DANCE OF DESIRE. If you'd like to find out how Caleb's buddy Danny Patterson got together with his new fiancée, buy DESIRE & ICE: A MacKenzie Family Novella, now available from all retailers. Here's a taste!

* * * *

She'd just give him one little kiss. Something to warm them, distract them and tide them over until they could be alone with all these explosive new feelings.

The next thing she knew she was on her back, their mouths locked, tongues finding their mutual rhythm. The thoughts flying through her head told her this was stupid, wrong. So what if he wasn't her student anymore, hadn't been for years.

They were still trapped. They should be watching the door, the window. They should be doing anything other than discovering they kissed like they were born to kiss each other. He broke suddenly, gazing into her eyes, shaking his head slowly as if he as if he were as dazed by this sudden burst of passion as she was.

"I think…" he tried, but lost his words.

"What do you think, Danny?"

"I think if we just keep our eyes on the door, we'll be fine."

"Okay."

Was he putting the brakes on? She wasn't sure. It was the most sensible thing to do, that was for sure. He slid off her and sat up, back against the wall, eyes on the door. She did the same. But he curved an arm around her back and brought her body sideways against his. It was awkward at first, but then he positioned her so that she was lying halfway across his lap.

"Now that I'm watching the door," he said, unbuttoning the top few buttons of her blouse, "I think we'll be fine."

"Oh, yeah?"

He brought his fingers to his mouth, moistened them with his tongue, then dipped them between the folds of her shirt. Slowly, he wedged them under the cup of her bra. When he found her nipple underneath, he said, "Yeah. Just fine."

In an instant, her body was flush with goose bumps.

Eyes on the door, his gun within reach, he circled her nipple with his moistened fingers. His precision and restraint combined to make her wet in other places as well. She'd seen the passion in his eyes, a youthful crush that had matured into a man's desire. But now, he was willing to delay his own gratification so that he could protect her and pleasure her at the same time.

"Let me give you a little help there," she whispered."